A GIFT FOR THE
DOCTOR

SARA FIELDS

Published by Stormy Night Publications and Design, LLC.
www.StormyNightPublications.com

Cover design by Korey Mae Johnson
www.koreymaejohnson.com

Images by Bigstock/Forplayday and 123RF/Ruslan Nassyrov

1st Print Edition. April 2016

ISBN-13: 978-1532945793

ISBN-10: 1532945795

CHAPTER ONE

Morgana squeezed her eyes shut, hoping to wake up from this terrible dream. Unfortunately, when she opened her eyes again, she was still on her back on the medical table, and the strange man was gazing back at her, all the while observing her and seemingly evaluating her reaction to him. She narrowed her eyes, suspicious of his every move. They stared at each other, neither backing down.

"Who are you," she whispered defiantly, enforcing some false sense of bravado in her voice, when all she felt was fear and some sort of feeling that she could only identify as desire, edging up from the tips of her toes. Her nipples peaked, and she remembered that she was completely naked and bound to a metal examination table. Her thighs quivered at the thought, the metal cooling to her skin. She tried to push that awareness from her mind, so that she could focus on the situation at hand, but the longer he gazed upon her naked body, the more difficulty she had finding her focus.

The man looked back at her, his white lab coat shifting as he leaned on the counter behind him. As he uncrossed his arms, she watched him with curiosity. He was tall, and very large for a man. She knew he probably wasn't human, but an Erassan, an alien race that inhabited the planet of Terranovum. Many Erassans had different abilities. Some had the gift of mental powers, whereas others had abilities that even she didn't know anything about. There was something about the deep yellow of his eyes told her this was probably one of those ancient species of Erassan, and she had no idea what he was capable of.

He wore a pair of dark blue jeans and a black t-shirt under his white lab coat. Morgana licked her lips when she saw that a hint of chest hair framed the V-neck of his collar. The dark fabric did little to hide the bulge of strength underneath, hugging the sculpted edges of tight chest muscles. His stomach was lean, tapering down to a trim waist. His features oozed power, confidence, and most surprisingly, dominance. She felt her mouth become dry, her body beginning to truly betray her. She suddenly wanted to see what was underneath all that clothing and the thought startled her. All the while, he watched her as she studied him. Strong angles cut his jawline, shadowed by stubble and a soft hint of a smile.

"You can call me Kade," he said, finally responding to her question. His voice was rugged and firm, yet strangely gentle.

"Where am I," she pressed further, breaking eye contact in order to further examine her surroundings.

The room reminded her much of the doctor's offices back on Earth, yet this one seemed more sterile, as though it only had a singular purpose, her examination. The walls were lined with silver steel and the floor was a dark office tile. There was nothing on the walls to provide any sort of warmth or color. One round window allowed natural light to filter into the room, but upon further observation, she saw set-in lights in the ceiling, all centered on the examination table she was bound to. Shifting, she tested her restraints again, but they didn't give her any leeway.

Her arms were bound over her head and she was lying on her back. Her bottom was positioned near the end of the table and her feet lay flat on its surface, her toes gripping the edge. She blushed as she realized how very much she was on display for him as she waited for him to answer her.

"You're in the D'Lormere capital of Drentine. Lord Nero brought you here in order for me to fully examine you, to study your abilities as a sorceress, and to confirm that you could indeed bear children."

"What? You can't possibly be serious." Morgana asked, dumbfounded.

Closing her eyes in disbelief, she finally remembered what had happened. In order to save the city of Eridell and her friends, she had offered herself in exchange as a captive. If a little reluctantly, she had agreed to the trade for the safety of her people, her king, and especially Emma and Lana. By giving herself up to the enemy, she had saved them all from whatever Nero had planned for them. She was here to find the enemy's weakness. She had chosen this, and she would have to bear whatever the enemy was going to do to her before she had a chance to escape. Even as a prisoner in the enemy territory, she could help King Dante, no matter what it took. If there were a way to destroy the enemy from the inside, she would find it. Her resolve back in full force, she opened her eyes and glared back at him.

She watched him silently as he picked up his clipboard and began to move closer toward her, his gait purposeful. Whatever he was going to do to her, it was about to begin. Squirming nervously, she tried to loosen her ties once again, but to no avail. Before she knew it, his large frame was standing beside her, and she felt her pussy clench in response to his proximity. He was very nice to look at.

A shiver raced down her spine as she watched him. He wrote down a few notes before putting them down on the counter. When he turned back to her, his face had a look of calm determination.

She was strong. *I can do this*, she thought to herself.

His gaze lingered up and down her body, before rough fingertips touched and glided over her smooth skin. The tiny hairs on her flesh rose skyward at his touch, and gooseflesh prickled all over her body. A sudden surge of desire raced through her veins, along with a requisite feeling of confusion. Her brow furrowed in response.

Slowly, his palm flattened over her stomach, pressing down firmly and calmly assessing her response. Palpating her lower abdomen, he looked back at her—for any signs of pain, she guessed—but then he quickly moved on. His eyes flicked to meet hers again. Seemingly satisfied with her torso, he moved his hands up toward her breasts.

Morgana fought against her bonds as his fingers edged closer to the hard peaks of her nipples. Her limbs tight against the leather cuffs, there was no possibility of escape. A soft whine escaped her throat.

Taking her nipples between his thumb and forefinger, he rolled and pinched the pebbled points of her breasts. She gasped as sensation ricocheted throughout her body, desire firmly beginning to pump through her veins, and felt her peaks tighten further, almost impossibly, painfully so. Breathing deep, she tried to sort out all the heightened arousal that her body was determined to feel.

He palmed her breasts, thoroughly inspecting every inch of them, while Morgana writhed underneath him. A profound sense of need and urgency began to pulse deep in her core as she felt wetness begin to pool between her thighs.

Kade examined her neck and her arms next, massaging her muscles as he continued his work. He paused when he reached one of her wrists, hesitantly touching the metal bracelet that hung heavily on her arm. Staring up at it, she remembered what it was.

Lord Nero had placed that bracelet there. It was an ancient object that possessed magical powers, and effectively silenced her abilities as a sorceress. She had become a powerful witch ever since the day she had set foot on Terranovum, and because of that, she had always known freedom in her daily life. When the Erassans of Legeari had realized the full extent of her magic, they had given her the role of the king's sorceress. There had been no higher honor for a human on Terranovum. This bracelet tore all of that away from her. She was nothing but a normal human girl now, with no powers to protect her from danger, and she felt as though a part of her was missing. Feeling entirely vulnerable, she shivered a little.

Now she was deep in enemy territory, bound to a table, and being examined for her worth by a strange man. Life wasn't fair.

She was jolted out of her thoughts as his palm grazed over her nipple once again, and her body soared with sudden sensation. A soft sigh escaped her lips as a wave of pleasure passed through her.

Her lower half quivered, anticipating his touch as he continued further down her body and she wasn't disappointed when he finally touched her there. His fingertips brushed the tiny triangle of red hair between her legs, and her body reacted wickedly, her hips rising up, almost begging for him to touch her further. She felt a blush creep up her face when she realized how she had behaved, shamed at her body's wanton reaction.

Morgana knew that at any moment, he would find the irrefutable evidence of her arousal. Feeling herself blush, she could sense her wetness as it dripped onto her inner thighs.

As soon as he touched her aching pussy, his fingers slid across her nether lips, dewed with the dampness of her desire, Morgana arched her back, assaulted with strong shooting tendrils of lust. Up and down, he stroked her lips, and she trembled with the fire that burned underneath her skin, her hips rolling to meet his tempo.

Losing all sense of propriety, she moaned softly. She was ashamed to say she wanted more, craved more of his calm, assertive, and unmistakably dominant touch. The throbbing ache between her thighs continued to grow until it completely overwhelmed her.

She could hardly think; all she could do was feel.

"You are extremely sexually responsive. This is very good."

When he took his fingers away from her, she nearly cried out in frustration. A groan of annoyance at the man's sudden disappearance was cut short as she quickly brought her lips together, shocked at her reaction to his absence. Looking around, she realized he was fishing something out of a drawer, and opened her eyes wide when she realized what it was.

It was a speculum. She hadn't seen one in years, not since her days back on Earth. She gulped in nervousness and fidgeted on the table.

"Please don't," she whispered softly.

"I must, in order to assess if your body can handle a child. I will lubricate the instrument, but, seeing how wet you are, I shouldn't even have to."

Morgana blushed as she felt her insides clench at his observation. He could see everything, and a sense of shame came over her, but her arousal grew impossibly stronger. A whine escaped her lips as he came closer.

Kade put the speculum down on a small table next to her, and sat down in a chair that put him on the same level as her pussy. She glared at the metal tool for a moment before turning her eyes to watch him. He pulled on a pair of gloves and began to lubricate the medical instrument. Before long, she felt the cool metal touching her skin, and then it slipped inside her slick channel with such ease. Her face had to be as red as an apple. Groaning in embarrassment, she looked away toward the window.

"Good girl," he said, his voice filled with what sounded like pride.

Morgana felt his finger enter her through the speculum, and then squirmed as she sensed a strange prodding at what must have been her cervix. Everything he was doing to her was making her body sing with desire, however reluctantly she fought with her mind.

After a few short moments of additional probing, he took the medical instrument out of her and placed it back on the small table. She sighed with relief, hearing him remove his gloves with a snap.

Only it wasn't over. His fingers returned to the skin of her thighs, reaching back toward her pussy, only this time he took his ungloved palm and pressed it up against the heat radiating from her core. Quivering at this mark of ownership, she waited almost breathlessly, nervously anticipating what he was going to do next.

Kade's thumb began to circle her pulsating clit, and Morgana nearly fell apart at the intensity of the flood of lust that overcame her with his gentle caress. The rest of his fingers continued to stroke her moist lips, persistently coaxing her toward the edge into a world of pleasure. He played her body like a well-tuned instrument, as though he knew exactly where to touch in order to drive her insane with desire. After all the incredible feelings of need that her examination had brought forth so far, she knew she wouldn't be able to keep herself from orgasm for very long. Panting, she felt a soft sheen of sweat begin to coat her body.

Her hips reached toward him and almost as if rewarding her, he slipped one finger and then another inside her wanting pussy. Once he began to massage her inner walls, along with his still attending thumb on her clit, her orgasm finally broke over her. Her entire body tightened with her release, muscles tense with the ferocity of the extreme pleasure that raged inside her.

Her moans increased with frantic desire as she writhed under his touch, and the throbbing need inside her seemed to grow to dizzying proportions. All at once, it seemed like her world fractured and her body sang. Her orgasm seemed to go on forever and ever, an endless blaze igniting fireworks throughout her body, all the way down to her fingers and toes.

Finally, her body simply smoldered with the aftershocks

of her release. With a sigh of relief, Morgana allowed herself to just breathe.

She lay limp on the metal table, held steady by the taut leather cuffs that bound her ankles and wrists. Meekly, she lifted her eyes to meet his, and saw something deep within those yellow irises, something that looked animalistic, but strangely satisfied. He looked pleased with her reaction, when all she felt was shame for her body's wicked and wanton response.

Suddenly, a dangerous look came over his face, and a smirk played at the corners of his lips. He removed his hand from in between her legs, drifting his fingertips across the trembling flesh of her inner thighs until his caress grazed against her bottom cheeks.

Morgana tried to squeeze her legs shut, but her ankles were bound too far apart. He had complete access to every inch of her, and from the look on his face, he knew it. A whimper emerged from her throat as he continued to explore the curves of her bottom, before he began to part her cheeks. Her eyes went wide in response. What was he going to do next? He couldn't mean to touch her there, could he?

His forefinger touched the rim of her bottom hole and she gasped. No one had ever touched her there. Her mind told her she shouldn't enjoy it and that it should be utterly shameful, but her body was telling her something different, that it was oddly compelling instead of terrible. Hesitant, she focused on what she was beginning to feel develop between her legs, her arousal becoming clearer by the second as her clit pulsed in response to his touch.

Kade circled her tight rosette, all the while spreading her wetness around it. She tried to close her eyes, but Kade's voice echoed around her.

"I want to see your eyes when I take you here, keep them open."

"Or else what," she challenged back, her voice wavering with what she could only identify as desire.

His eyes narrowed, a stern, but slightly amused look coming over him that dared her to push him. His finger invaded her bottom as he leaned close to her. He pushed the tip inside and then pulled it out, over and over until her legs began to quiver. As much as she tried not to, her hips rolled to meet his thrusts, and an unquenched fire begin to flare once again deep in her core.

"Or else I will have to take these cuffs off you, bend you over this table, and give you the spanking you deserve for disobeying me. Are you sure you still want to test me?"

Speechless, she stared back at him and shook her head. He pressed his finger deeper inside her bottom hole and watched her. She felt shock at his invasion, embarrassed at her body's wicked reaction, and full in a way she had never felt before. With his other hand, he began to rub her aching bud. It pulsed underneath his touch, and she felt her need begin to grow once again, but this time it felt stronger, and came rushing back with such ferocity that her desire for him to take her completely nearly overwhelmed her.

Throwing her head back, Morgana arched on the table as a second, much more powerful orgasm crashed through her. Her bottom pulsed around his fingers, and she panted with her shame and want. She had never had someone touch her there before, hadn't even known she'd wanted it. Wildly, she rolled her hips against his touch, rubbing his finger against her clit and taking him deeper into her bottom. Desperate moans sounded as she rode the wave of pleasure until she lay spent, claimed by his hand on her pussy and the penetration of his finger inside her bottom.

When he finally removed his hand from her, she felt suddenly empty, bereft and lonely for his touch.

She trembled on the table. Kade began to massage the muscles in her legs, finishing his assessment of her body, all the while caressing her skin. No longer did she try to fight him; instead, she enjoyed his simple, dominating touch.

Watching him, she saw a certain hunger develop in his gaze. He looked at her almost like she was his prey, and he, a predator. Her chest rose and fell with her breath as she waited for whatever he wanted to do next.

She was disappointed when he turned away and picked up his clipboard, writing down notes as his back was to her. Her feelings of pleasure ebbed away, and she began to feel chilled.

"Kade?" she whispered softly. He turned back to her, putting his clipboard back on the counter.

"Can I have a blanket? I'm cold," she said, as a shiver raced down her spine.

He opened a cabinet and pulled out a dark blue fleece comforter. Putting it down next to her, he took her wrist and unclasped it from the cuffs that held her tight. Reaching for her other hand and then her ankles, he freed her one limb at a time.

She sat up so that her legs hung over the edge, and he draped the blanket around her shoulders. Clutching it close, she huddled in its warmth.

"Now that I have untied you, remember you must be on your best behavior. I won't hesitate to redden that little bottom of yours until it matches the hair on your head."

Narrowing her eyes, she took in his no-nonsense demeanor and decided to test him a bit. There was no way he was being serious. He wouldn't actually spank her, would he?

"You wouldn't dare."

"Try me. Lord Nero gave me permission to do whatever I need to do to get you to cooperate. And if that means putting you over my knee? I can certainly make that happen."

Morgana pulled the blanket closer around herself, almost as though it was a shield. She had never submitted to anyone in her life, and wasn't about to. Raising her chin with as much attitude as she could muster, she glared back at him. She was the king's sorceress, a woman to be respected and revered. Her station had made sure she was always taken care of and never wanted for anything.

There was no way in hell she'd bow down to this arrogant doctor. Not today, and not any other day.

"Don't you dare lay a hand on me. I am Morgana, sorceress to King Dante, and you will respect me. I am not a force to be trifled with," she said, her voice strong and unafraid as she challenged him.

Kade simply moved closer to her, his body towering over hers. He put his hands on the table on either side of her and leaned in toward her face, a dangerous smirk playing at his lips. She leaned backwards, trying to keep a respectable distance between the two of them, despite the events that had just occurred between them on that very table.

"Are you trying to test me, little girl?"

Morgana kept silent, staring him down. She wasn't about to back down to him, not to anyone. No matter what happened, her pride was at stake.

Kade pushed his hands off the table and backed a step away from her. At first she thought she had won, but the words that came out of his mouth next had her legs feeling like jelly.

"Get up."

"What?" she answered, her voice faltering.

"Get up off the table. Don't make me say it again," he ordered, placing a hand firmly on her shoulder.

"Don't touch me!" she yelled back, trying to pull herself out of his grasp.

He sighed at her defiance, and before she knew it, he had lifted her off the table and sat down in her place. It all happened so fast that she had no time to react as he put her face down over his knees. His left hand gripped her hips, and his leg snaked over hers so that she was effectively restrained without a chance of escaping. She couldn't even kick her legs.

Whipping back her head, she tried in vain to push herself off of him. Feeling entirely vulnerable at this unexpected position, she recognized how bare and how completely unprotected her sensitive nether cheeks were. She jolted at his touch when he placed his hand on her bottom. Gasping, she realized just how large his hands were, covering what felt like the entirety of one of her cheeks. Suddenly, she was very nervous at her decision to test his patience and bordered on regretting it altogether.

"Now. Are you ready to listen to me?"

"I can't believe the nerve..."

Smack! Smack! Smack!

The sound of spanks filled her ears before she realized he had paddled her with his palm. In a second, the sting caught her by surprise, crawling across her skin like she had just been stung by hundreds of bees. His hand came down again and again on either side until her entire backside was beginning to burn. Trying to wriggle out of his grasp, she tried to cover her bottom with her hands. Kade grabbed her wrists and pinned them to her back, effectively keeping her from any shenanigans.

His spanks became fiercer and much harsher, the bite of each one sinking deep into her reddening bottom. He spanked all over her backside as she continually tried to fight him, until he began the next series of smacks on her upper thighs. He focused on spanking the very sensitive area where her bottom and thighs met, and Morgana felt a cry escape her lips. She couldn't believe how much this punishment was beginning to hurt. Feeling tears come to her eyes, she tried to hold them back but couldn't help it as one escaped down her cheek. Soon, tears were streaming down her face in earnest.

The spanking seemed to last forever, until Morgana was sobbing in remorse for her decision. She was sure the entirety of her bottom was red, along with her punished thighs. Kade placed his hand on her poor aching globes and she flinched in response.

"Now, Morgana, are you going to behave? And before you respond, remember that this spanking can continue with my belt if need be."

"Yes, I'll behave," she responded, sniffling as her tears began to dry. There was no way she wanted to feel the lick of his belt against her already tortured buttocks.

He spanked her again, one harsh smack to each side and she yelped at the sudden sting biting into her already sore nether cheeks.

"'Yes, sir' is the correct answer. Let me hear you say it."

"Yes, sir," she said softly.

"Louder," he said sternly, spanking her yet again.

"Please! Yes, sir!" she cried out, desperate for him to stop. If he continued to punish her anymore, she feared her bottom would fall off. Kade let go of her arms and helped her into a sitting position on his lap. Gently, he wiped away her tears with his thumbs, grasped her chin, and quietly stared into her eyes.

"I'm sorry, sir," she whispered, her voice barely audible.

"Good girl," he said, and a strange sense of pride burned through her. It was then she noticed the throb developing between her legs, and the wetness that was beginning to slick across her pussy lips. She swallowed hard at this realization, embarrassed at her body's betrayal. Her bottom still incredibly sore, she wondered how she could possibly be turned on by a spanking that hurt that much.

Cautiously, she allowed her hands to move toward his chest, where her fingertips met the cool white material of his coat. Feeling the muscles of his upper body and shoulders through the fabric of his clothes, her breath hitched and her body began to burn hotter with desire for him. There was something about sitting in his lap, him completely clothed and her totally naked with a burning bottom, that left her blushing with shame, yet wanting more.

She felt her state of arousal grow to new heights, and tried to cinch her legs together so that the evidence would be hidden from him. Unfortunately, as soon as she shifted her legs, his eyes dropped to her lower body. His hand moved to trace up the length of her skin to the cleft between her legs. When she refused to open them for him, he lightly smacked the top of her thigh.

"Open your legs," he commanded, his tone gentle, yet unyielding. Morgana sighed with embarrassment as she forced herself to comply, not wanting another dose of his over the knee treatment. She knew what he was about to find, and whined when his fingers discovered just how wet she was.

"Morgana," he said, surprise clear in his voice. "It seems you have enjoyed your spanking a little bit, hmmmm?"

She felt a wicked blush creep over her cheeks, shamed at her body's unrestrained response. Hiding her face in his shoulder, she gasped as he began to spread her juices all over her aching pleasure bud.

Her hips began to move to meet the roll of his fingertips, and she moaned into his shirt. It didn't take long for her to begin writhing and panting at his firm touch, his dominating presence taking over her senses in the most delicious way.

Shuddering with pleasure, she rode his fingers until her orgasm flared through her system, racing through her with such fiery passion and intensity that it surprised even her. Collapsing against him, she moaned as powerful aftershocks surged deep in her muscles and throughout her body. Kade held her close as she worked through the sensations that continually assaulted her.

It took her long moments to recover.

"I don't know why I reacted like that," she finally whispered, confused about the strong feelings that were bouncing around inside her head and all over every inch of her anatomy. She breathed a sigh of relief when she finally began to feel normal again, her face flushing at the thought of what she had just done with a man she hardly even knew.

Kade silently observed her, his yellow eyes gentle and warm as she curled into his embrace.

"I'm going to tell you something now, Morgana, and you have to promise me that you are going to remain calm. Can you do that for me?"

Confused, she lifted her head, looking back at him. Slowly she nodded, a soft dread edging in from the recesses of her mind.

"Lord Nero has charged me with your care. He will check in on you now and again, but he has requested that my bloodline be paired with yours so that our children may serve his needs."

"What!?" she cried out, pushing away from him. "He plans to breed me? You can't even begin to think I would be alright with this!"

"Morgana, calm down."

Seething, she climbed off his lap and began to pace in front of him. She couldn't believe what he had just told her. She was so used to dictating her own life, and this threw her for a loop. Lord Nero didn't have the right to use her like this. She may be his hostage, but that didn't mean he could do with her what he wanted.

"Morgana…"

"What!?" she fired back. Immediately, she regretted her outburst as he stood up, his large frame towering over her. Taking a step back, she looked up at him as butterflies tumbled through her belly.

"Don't make me spank you for a second time today."

"Sorry, sir," she murmured softly, unable to break his gaze. Her ire simmered to a low glow, and then burnt out into nothingness. Nervously, she fidgeted and tried to act as confidently as she dared, beginning to feel a little scared that he would take her without her consent.

"Are you going to do it now? Take me here, against my will, on this table?"

"No. You can relax, Morgana. I won't ever force you. I promise you that. I will take you back to my cabin though, so that you may unwind and rest somewhere more comfortable."

"Is your cabin like this place?" she asked, her eyes looking around apprehensively.

"No. We're in one of the many buildings devoted to

D'Lormere technology. This is one of the medical facilities in our city."

Morgana felt her lips form a silent 'o,' and she absentmindedly touched her bottom. Blushing, she felt the heat radiating off her punished cheeks, and lifted her eyes to watch Kade's reaction. He was smiling at her.

"I have a feeling that you are going to have a red bottom very often, until you learn to mind what I say."

She glared back at him, then turned away so she couldn't see his look of pride at her juvenile chastisement.

"You're to wear the human slave attire when we travel to my home. You will wait here as I go and fetch one. Make sure you behave. I have ways of punishing you that will leave you trembling with a red bottom, sore in more ways than one. Is that clear?"

"Yes, sir," she mumbled begrudgingly, hoping to please him with an acquiescent tone. As soon as he walked out that door, she would be looking around the room for something, anything she could use to escape or take down the D'Lormerean Empire. She tried with all her might to keep her face devoid of all emotion, so that she could keep her intentions secret.

"Do I need to restrain you again?" he asked, his eyes assessing her for mischief.

"No, sir. I'll behave," she said softly, keeping her eyes on the floor, looking as demure and innocent as she could possibly muster. Hearing the click of the door, she breathed a sigh of relief and looked up, making sure the coast was clear. Quickly, she rushed to the door to check to see if it opened. To her dismay, it was already locked.

Next, she made her way over to the window, in order to take in her surroundings and to learn about Drentine.

She had been told stories about the city of Drentine, the capital of the enemy territory D'Lormere, but she had never seen it in person herself. Rumors foretold of a city that was so technologically advanced, using up stores of dark matter, the planet's energy source, at a much more rapid place than the rest of the world. Seeing the city now in front of her, she was sure Drentine used much more dark matter in a few hours than the entire kingdom of Legeari did in a month.

King Dante would be appalled at the sight.

She was at the apex of a very tall building, yet others still towered over her. Nightfall had taken place, and she could see the stars and moons overhead. Lights flickered all around her, both inside and outside of all the structures she could see. From what she could make out, the lights weren't powered by magic, as they looked similar to light bulbs that she had witnessed back on Earth. Small airships flew by fairly regularly, but at an alarmingly high number. The sheer amount of dark matter needed to power this place must be staggering. To keep up with demand, Drentine must be sending out cargo ships every day in order to power everything that required dark matter to function.

She had seen some of the kingdom of D'Lormere a short time ago, when she had traveled to their camp not far outside of Legeari. She had gone in order to rescue Lana from the clutches of Lord Nero, who had captured the poor girl. The surrounding territories had been poverty stricken, so much so that even the Erassans suffered and not just the human population. The difference between the capital and the outside settlements was staggering. The wealthy here had all the luxuries in the world while the poor people who lived outside the city suffered with nothing. Just the thought made Morgana feel a little sick to her stomach.

Sitting back on the table, she watched the comings and goings of the people living in the technology-laden oasis. With ever-increasing dread, she wondered just how Legeari would conquer such a major, technology-driven city. Despair rattled through her body and a tear rolled down her cheek. How was she, a simple human girl now that she had been robbed of her abilities, supposed to deal a crushing blow to the enemy when it seemed that they had every advantage in the world?

A large hand touched her shoulder gently, but she

jumped away in shock. Her heart pounding in her chest, she turned to see that Kade had already returned. She hadn't even heard the door open. Looking down at his arms, she saw the telltale red sheer garment that marked a human slave, which was soon to mark her as one as well.

Looking up at her face, concern crossed over his features. He put the outfit aside on the table and stood in front of her.

"Morgana, is there something wrong?" he asked, wiping her tears from her cheeks with his thumbs, grasping her chin in the process.

"No, sir. Nothing's wrong."

"Lying to me is grounds for punishment, Morgana. I don't take kindly to it."

"I don't even know you."

He pursed his lips in response and turned away. His reaction chilling, she shivered, still afraid of him and what he could do to her. Coldly, he helped her to stand, and dressed her in the sheer red outfit. When he finished, he took something out of his pocket and clipped it around her throat. It was a wide leather collar, with a metal loop at the front. With another clasping sound, she realized he had also attached her to a leash. Rage simmered within her, before she did her best to quell it. If she was smart, she would just have to wait until he dropped his guard, and then maybe she could escape or figure out a way to fatally hurt Lord Nero along the way. But, she had to remember that Kade was one of them, one of the people who threatened her home and her king.

CHAPTER TWO

Kade escorted Morgana by the leather leash out of the examination room and into the hallway. He didn't jerk her forward, but instead led her calmly down the stark corridor, allowing her to keep pace with him.

She didn't question the collar and the leash; she knew why he found the need to use it. He didn't trust her, and she didn't trust him. No matter that he made her body jump at his touch, crave it even, he was still a member of the enemy. He reported to Lord Nero, one of the slimiest, most horrifying men she had ever had the chance to know. She also knew nothing about Kade. He was a mystery. His yellow eyes hinted at abilities she couldn't even guess at. Who knew if when they arrived at his cabin, he wouldn't throw her on his bed and claim her as his without her consent? He could just as easily be lying to her too.

If he wanted to, he certainly could take her. It was a terrifying thought. Would he take from her what she wasn't ready to give? For all she knew, he was trying to get into her head, so that he could tell Lord Nero all he knew. She would have to be careful, especially in what she told him about herself and her home kingdom of Legeari, and especially what she told him about King Dante.

SARA FIELDS

Following him, she tried to keep her resolve strong so that she didn't falter. Watching him saunter away, never looking back at her, she narrowed her eyes. She wouldn't fall for his dubious antics, no matter how much her body craved him.

His back muscles were tense underneath his clothes, and he walked with such purpose that she struggled to keep up. He led her to an elevator before guiding her in silently without so much a glance. He pressed the first floor button and looked straight ahead, not meeting her questioning gaze. By the time they reached the first floor, she was beginning to get annoyed.

He led her across the floor of the first story of the building, outside into the cool night air. From there, he hailed a passing airship, which stopped so fast that Morgana nearly ran backwards in order to escape. The leash pulled hard on her collar, and she froze, wild panic slowly disappearing from her eyes. Slowly, Kade turned to face her, his features softening at her terrified reaction.

Gently, he took her hand and led her into the small ship. There was a seating area in the back, large enough for two or three people. Kade drew her in beside him, and she begrudgingly allowed him. Feeling his warmth, she closed her eyes and pretended he was someone else, someone from Legeari, who would support her service to the king and Lana.

Opening her eyes and glancing up at him, she knew, at that moment, that he wasn't that person, and it would take a hell of a lot of convincing to change his mind. She noticed he was looking at her too, his eyes a strange mix of ice and warmth. What was his deal? Finally, when she felt like she couldn't take it anymore, she whispered into the silence.

"Kade? Are you angry with me?"

"Morgana, when I ask you a question, I expect an honest answer."

"I couldn't. I don't know you, nor can I trust you."

"Well, with time, I hope to change that. Until then, I still expect you to be honest with me at all times."

She looked back up at him, meeting his eyes. He was a mystery to her, a strange man who had been given responsibility for her captivity. Still, she didn't quite know if she could trust him. He seemed kind, if not fair, and she couldn't help but blush at the memories of what he had done to her on that metal table. Her body growing hot, she had a hard time quelling the attraction she felt for him.

Looking away, she couldn't be sure if he wouldn't turn her in to Lord Nero at the slightest bit of information about her home. She made a vow to herself to remember that he was the enemy, no matter what he said to her and how much her body yearned for him.

Before she knew it, the ship was coming to an abrupt stop. Kade held her close to him in order to keep her from jerking forward. He helped her out of the small ship, taking her arm until she was settled on the ground. Gently tugging on the leash, he led her into a small building. It was two stories high and made up of mostly glass windows, but strangely enough, she couldn't see inside. Upon further inspection, she realized the glass was mirrored.

He led her into the front door, locking it behind her. Looking around at the entryway, it was clear she was looking at a bachelor pad. There wasn't a feminine touch in sight. Everything was neat and put together well, but she got a distinct simple and stark impression from the place.

"Is this your home?" she asked, her voice soft.

"Yes."

"Is anyone here with you?"

"No, I live alone."

"What do you plan to do with me?"

There was little she could do to keep her nerves from edging into her voice. He turned back to her, his gaze softening a little. Moving toward her, her unclipped the leash from her neck, but the leather collar still hung heavy on her throat. His fingers grazed against the skin of her chin, and it took everything she had not to lean into his touch.

"Are you hungry?"

"What?"

"When was the last time they fed you?"

"I… I don't remember."

"Come on. Follow me," he said, walking further down the hall. Following him, she realized he had led her into some form of a kitchen. It looked similar to one from her days on Earth, but there were a few things she didn't recognize. She first noticed that there was no oven or fridge like in a traditional kitchen. There were plenty of light gray cabinets, and a beautiful countertop made of a dark gray rock with veins of white snaking through it, which matched the cool smoky color of the tile floor. It was an extremely modern-looking kitchen, but clean and decidedly masculine.

"Where is your food?" she asked timidly, still looking around.

"I don't cook. I bought a meal synthesizer long ago. You simply tell it what you want to eat and it will make it for you." He pointed at a large, square metal box on the counter that looked much like a microwave, but with much more complicated controls.

"A meal synthesizer? I've never heard of such a thing."

"You mean you don't have them in Eridell?"

"I have never seen one. Does it use a lot of energy?"

"I'm not sure. Maybe."

"Doesn't Lord Nero limit your use of dark matter?"

"No. Never in my time here."

"Have you always lived here, Kade? I mean, have you ever been outside the city and seen what it's like?"

With a heavy sigh, he looked back at her, his eyes meeting hers, yet somewhere still seeming like he was far away.

"I used to live on the border of Legeari and D'Lormere. When I was very young, the D'Lormerean army raided my town. My father was killed trying to protect us, and my mother was forced onto an airship. I never saw her again. They took me as well, only they placed me in a medical training program and I've been here ever since."

"I'm sorry," she whispered, her voice barely audible.

"I know what it's like out there. I know how different it is. The people living here have no qualms about wasting anything, but for many people, it's because they feel that the capital owes them something. In my case, D'Lormere killed my family."

"I didn't know," she said, her voice lingering.

"I know. Legeari was once my home. You have more allies than you think here in the capital. My people knew you were coming; there were whispers about a great sorceress prisoner to be trained and bred by us for Lord Nero's use. I made sure he was aware of my presence and that I was perfectly willing to take you in hand, and as a result, he ended up giving you to me."

Morgana looked back at him, assessing his eyes in order to figure out if he was telling her the truth. There was not even the slightest hint of a lie in his eyes. Still, she felt reluctant to trust him based on a simple story, even if it tore at her heart just a little. She had seen his sadness, and felt the loss of his family through his words.

Regardless of what Kade said, Lord Nero had still trusted him to keep her prisoner, to watch over her, and most worrisome of all, to breed her. She couldn't rely on him.

Dropping her eyes to the floor, she wrung her hands, choosing not to respond to his revelation. She heard him begin to open cabinets and heard her stomach growl. Giggling, she pressed her fingers to her stomach, almost as though her touch could stop the sound from being heard.

Blushing furiously, she looked up at Kade. A smirk hinted at his lips as he turned away toward the meal synthesizer.

"What would you like to eat?"

"Anything I want?"

"Yes, whatever you like. I can program whatever I'm craving into it and it will be ready in just minutes. It's really incredible."

"Even Earth things?"

"Actually, it does make things from there. What would you like?"

"I would love a plate of lasagna. I haven't had that in the longest time," she said almost shyly. She watched as he pressed a few buttons on the keyboard.

"Coming right up." The machine whirred to life, humming softly for a few seconds before quieting down. Kade opened the door to the contraption, and removed a steaming hot plate of lasagna that looked freshly cooked, drizzled with sauce and a sprinkling of Parmesan cheese. Morgana felt her stomach growl even louder as she breathed in the delicious aroma. He put the plate on the large wooden table in the center of the kitchen, and pulled out a chair for her.

"Sit." She obeyed without question, her mouth watering at the sight of the food. He retrieved silverware and a napkin for her, and she dug right in.

He returned moments later with what looked like a large steak, some sort of green vegetable native to Terranovum, and a potato. Sitting down in the seat across from her, he took a small bite of meat before looking up at her, his expression one of curiosity.

"Tell me about yourself. You're from Earth, right?"

"Yes. I am."

"Well, what was your life there like?"

Morgana watched him for a moment before deciding it was a safe enough question for her to answer. She sat back and finished chewing a bite of her meal.

"I haven't been on Earth for over five years now. I used to live in the United States, on the east coast in Rhode Island. It's such a tiny little state. The city I lived in was called Providence. I had a mother and a father there, but we weren't terribly close. I had gone off to college in New Jersey and my father went off to try to start a career as a comedian, with my mom as his manager. They died in a car crash when I was seventeen. Dante found me late one night a year later wandering on the beach and I woke up in the holding cells. Fortunately, I wasn't there long. The Terranovum air had awakened something deep within my genetics, and I developed my magical powers. From there, I was appointed a very high position within the castle. For years now, I have helped watch over the city of Eridell and its people."

"I didn't realize you've been here on Terranovum for that long. It must feel awful after losing your powers to that bracelet."

She touched the heavy band on her wrist, its metal a constant reminder of what Lord Nero had taken from her. The intricate tribal markings around the bracelet inscribed a heavy spell, which locked down her magical abilities so that she had no access to them. She was nothing but a simple human girl without them.

He watched her closely, his eyes warm. Morgana almost felt safe for a moment, until she remembered that he was still an enemy.

She took the last few bites of her meal and sat back, feeling completely full. He finished his steak and moved onto the sides. Before long, he was finished, took their plates off the table, and put them in a device that looked much like the dishwashers she remembered back on Earth.

"Thank you. That lasagna was delicious. Just like the real thing!"

"I'm glad you liked it. You should get ready for bed though; it's been a long day. It makes my skin crawl knowing how you were likely treated in Lord Nero's care."

"I don't remember much. I do recall being pretty hungry for much of it. For some reason, I think they gave me some sort of sleeping drug in my water for the majority of the trip. I only remember small flashes of a cart early on, and then he loaded me onto a ship. I don't remember anything after that until I woke up on your table."

His face darkened, and he looked away for a moment

before turning back to her.

"All the more reason to get you tucked into bed. Come on, follow me."

"Where am I going to sleep?"

"In my bed."

"No, I can't do that," she answered firmly, the shock freezing her in her seat.

"You can, and you will. This is not up for discussion," he replied, his voice stern.

"Please, Kade, don't do this," she pleaded, her voice beginning to edge into fear. Was he about to force himself on her? Was this it?

He looked back at her, seemingly sensing her distress. His face softened, and he placed his hands on her shoulders.

"Morgana. I'm putting you in my bed so that I can keep watch over you. I would never force a woman to be with me, but I do hope, one day, that you will beg me to take you. But, that day will not be today."

"You promise you won't?"

"I will never break my word. I promise you, I will not force you in this."

"Thank you," she whispered as she felt relief pour over her. Kade dropped his hands from her shoulders and took her hand, gently prodding her to follow him. She looked down at his fingers, his broad hand swallowing up her much smaller one. He was so much bigger than she was, and he was even large for an Erassan male. She would have to take him at his word. No matter how much she fought, if he wanted to lay claim to her, he could, especially since she didn't have her powers to protect her.

They reached a door at the end of the hall and Kade opened it, leading her into his bedroom. He looked back at her before motioning her inside. Once the two of them entered the room, he helped her undress and Morgana didn't fuss, but watched him with a certain wariness that she couldn't hide. Before long, she was once again naked in his presence. He pointed to a door in the corner and told her that was the bathroom.

"Come. I will draw you a warm bath, and you can relax until bedtime."

Morgana padded after him into the bathroom, and was surprised by the warm red and beige colors that decorated the room. The largeness of the room surprised her. It had a shower, a toilet, and a set of double sinks. She gasped at the size of the bathtub, complete with a number of jets. She sat on the ledge while he fiddled with the water, testing the temperature and pouring in a variety of beautifully scented oils. When the water reached a high enough level, he turned it off and helped her to climb inside.

Groaning as the warm water enveloped her legs, she sank down into the tub. Once her body was fully covered, she leaned her head back as feelings of relaxation poured through her.

"You have one hour. I will return after that so that we can get you into bed."

"Yes, sir."

Looking back at him, she saw he was smiling at her, almost as though he was proud of her. She beamed back shyly, blushing at his response.

He turned on the jets and she moaned as they pounded into her sore muscles. This felt like heaven. Closing her eyes, she melted into the heat and the soothing pulse of the jets, and just let herself relax. After what felt like only a few moments, she forgot everything. She forgot how she was a prisoner in the enemy territory, about Lord Nero's cruelty, and how she was going to help King Dante destroy D'Lormere. At that minute, nothing else mattered but the warm water melting away her worries and the scents of the soothing oils Kade had poured into the bathwater.

She heard Kade come back into the room and opened her eyes to look up at him.

"Has it already been an hour?"

"Yes, it has. Did you enjoy yourself?"

"Yes, very much so. This tub is heavenly."

"Come, let me help you stand." He gripped her hand and assisted her as she climbed out of the tub, then wrapped her in warm towels as soon as she stepped out of the water. He picked her up and carried her back into the bedroom. Morgana was too weary to fight, and just let him. He placed her on the bed and rolled her onto her belly so he could take the towels off her.

His hands began to massage her all over, further melting her into a relaxed puddle of goo. She hardly noticed when he began to touch her bottom cheeks.

"Now that you're relaxed, Morgana, I'm going to give you some medicine to help you sleep, and some extra vitamins to boost your system after your journey here."

"Alright," she answered, looking back and extending her hand so that he might give her the pills to swallow, but he pushed her hand away. Instead, he parted her bottom cheeks and squeezed something cool against her tight rosette.

"What are you doing?"

Her buttocks clenched as she tried pushing herself up on the bed, but a few sharp spanks to her backside stopped her from going any further. She jerked a little when his thumb invaded her bottom hole, spreading something slippery around the rim. Feeling him begin to push a rounded object inside her, she whimpered until it popped into her bottom. With a whine, she realized it was a suppository.

Feeling her face flame in embarrassment, she hid it in the nearest pillow. He followed the suppository inside her with his finger, situating it deep inside her channel. She groaned as he followed the first one with a second, and then a third, until she felt impossibly full. After each one, he would insert his finger into her bottom hole to situate the capsule, making her blush each and every time.

Finally, once all three were inside her, he showed her a small purple butt plug.

"You will wear this so that your medicine will be fully absorbed inside you."

She didn't even have time to answer before she felt the tip of the plug nudge at the entrance of her bottom hole. He began to press it into her, the slippery fluid allowing it to slip inside her with ease. With a pop, it sat deep inside her tight little hole, ensuring that the suppositories would not slip out

With a start, she realized how warm her body had become, and she could feel her arousal beginning to moisten her thighs. How could something so shameful make her body react that way?

His fingers stroked across the flesh of her inner thighs, up toward her dampened nether lips. As soon as he made contact with her pussy, she moaned at the sensations that shot deep into her core.

He began to rub her clit, circling his fingers up and down, and then around until she was shaking with need, her desire beginning to overwhelm her.

"Do you think you deserve to have an orgasm?"

"Please, sir. Please," she begged, her voice sounding desperate, her hips following the deft movements of his fingers. He didn't answer her, but instead began to increase the pressure on her needy bud. She ground into his palm and cried out when he pinched the folds surrounding her clit.

"You may come for me, Morgana."

His words allowed the coil tight inside her to snap, as feelings of intense satisfaction took over her entire being. Her legs quivered as loud moans escaped her lips. He held his hand over her pussy until her body quieted, his touch incredibly possessive and delightfully firm.

"Thank you, sir," she whispered, her voice a bit hoarse.

"Let's get you settled into bed now. It's been a long day."

She allowed him to pull up the covers around her, and before she knew it, her eyes were drifting closed as sleep quickly overcame her. The last thing she remembered was the warm look on Kade's face as he sat on the bed beside her.

CHAPTER THREE

Kade watched as Morgana drifted off to sleep. She was naked and in his bed, her fire red hair cascading about the pillow. When she tossed around in her sleep, the sheet slid down her chest, revealing a taut little pink nipple, and he smiled. Moving closer, he pulled the blankets close around her so that she wouldn't catch a chill.

He remembered her wild eyes as she lay bound to the medical table, and he recalled how with but a simple touch, her body had succumbed to the raw pleasure he had awakened within her. Her long limber body, lean legs, and pert breasts were something that he would be unable to erase from his mind for a very long time. She was the most beautiful woman he had ever laid eyes on.

Remembering her stunning violet-colored eyes, he pushed a rebellious strand of hair out of her face. Those eyes told him a story of a woman who was used to taking charge, and in them he saw her struggle to submit to him, and the inner turmoil within her about whether to trust him.

Little did she know, he was actually on her side and wanted to take down Lord Nero as much as she did. For a very long time, he had bowed down to Lord Nero's cruelty and had waited for the right moment in order to exact his revenge. Morgana was a crucial part of that plan. He had been part of an underground group that existed outside the city walls for some time now. They had detailed plans in place, following the comings and goings of the dark matter cargo ships, of the plants that stored the energy source, and the security schedules of everyone involved in keeping it safe. All they needed was the touch of magic in order to succeed, and Morgana was the solution to that.

His gaze shifted to the heavy metal bracelet on her wrist, the awful thing that kept her powers in captivity. Somehow, he would need to figure out how to remove the wristlet if they were going to succeed. He looked at the tribal markings around the band, running his fingers along the designs. Something within those characters had to give a clue as to what it said; he just needed to understand what they meant. Maybe it was some form of ancient Erassan language, or a special dialect of some kind.

He would have to find someone who could read it, maybe someone who was magically inclined as well. His thoughts drifted to the stories he had heard of Eridell and the Hall of Magic. Maybe he would find the answer there.

Once he made sure Morgana was fully asleep, her breathing steady and even, he left the room and entered his study. Booting up his computer, a contraption that Terranovum scientists had discovered years ago, he began to research ancient Erassan dialects, specifically those connected with human magic. He read for a few more hours before returning to his room and curling up in bed with his redheaded sorceress. His mind was mottled with all sorts of information, none of it revealing the answer to his inquiry involving that wretched bracelet.

Pulling her up close to him, he marveled at her tiny size compared to his own. She fit right up against him, his larger body spooning her smaller one. His arm around her waist, he drifted off to sleep, wondering how he had ever slept alone when he could have had a soft woman to have and to hold, and to care for. How could things ever go back to being the same, now that he had met Morgana? Her pretty eyes, her saucy smile, and the delicious moans he had wrung out of her gorgeous limber body haunted his dreams.

• • • • • • •

A few hours later, morning broke and sunlight streamed in through the windows. Kade woke and detangled himself gently from Morgana, carefully to avoid jolting her from her sleep. He changed into a fresh set of clothes, made his way back into the kitchen, and prepared her a large portion of eggs, bacon, and toast. He wanted to make sure that she had plenty to eat so she would remain healthy. Heading into the bedroom, he sat beside her and gently shook her awake.

Groggily, Morgana opened her eyes, her violet irises bright against her pale skin. A soft, but slightly shy smile played at the edges of her lips as she saw him sit down next to her.

"Morning," she murmured softly, her voice still heavy with traces of sleep.

"I brought you breakfast."

"Mhhhmmm. I was wondering why I smelled the delicious scent of bacon on the air. I'm starving. Thank you." A soft blush crept up her face as she looked over at the plate, her desire for the food clear in her face. He handed her the platter and put a small table over her lap, something he had made himself for the purpose of having breakfast in bed. She placed the dish on the table and dug right in, thanking him again for thinking of her.

"When you're finished, please put on the clothing I gave you. We may venture out today so that I can show you some of the city. I want you to be aware of what is around us, so that you may stay safe."

"Yes, sir," she said softly, eyeing the sheer red human slave uniform placed over a nearby chair. She shivered. Noticing her chest was bare to his eyes, she pulled up the covers a little higher in order to shield herself.

"I'll be right down the hall. Call me if you need anything."

"Okay. I will. Thanks," she said while dropping her eyes, adding in a "sir" after a moment's pause.

Looking back at her for one last second, Kade finally turned away and exited the room. He went back into his study to see if he could find any more clues concerning the markings on the bracelet. Not long after, he heard little feet pad into the room and he raised his eyes to meet hers. He noticed the sheer red fabric hugging her curves, further highlighting her brilliant red hair. She looked the picture of a little firecracker.

"Kade?"

"Yes?"

"Am I to wear this plug in my bottom much longer?"

"No. Come here and bend over the table. Bare your bottom for me."

Shyly, as her face reddened adorably, she followed his instructions, revealing her gorgeous backside. She was a picture of submissive innocence as she bent over his desk, allowing the purple base of the plug to be seen between her tight cheeks. Grasping, he pulled it out slowly, and she gasped at the feeling. A loud pop sounded when the plug was finally free, and he heard her whine at the loss of it. He laughed slightly before allowing her to rise and cover herself.

He couldn't wait to take her there. His cock hardened at the thought. Trying to distract himself, his gaze fell to the hunk of metal at her wrist.

"Do you know anything about what that bracelet of yours might say?"

Lifting her arm, she stared down at the hunk of metal. Shaking her head, she looked back at him.

Taking a closer look, she studied the characters. "The text looks familiar; like I've seen it somewhere before in my reading." Pausing, her face twisted with concentration, and Kade couldn't help but smile at the sight.

"If only I could travel to the Hall of Magic, then I could look into the history archives. I think I vaguely remember something like it there…"

"Do you know much about that place?"

"It used to be my home. I would walk its halls every day."

A loud knock sounded on the door, startling the two of them with its ferocity. Kade rose from his heavy dark wooden desk and walked toward the door.

"You are not to speak unless spoken to. Is that clear?"

"Yes, sir," she replied a bit timidly, a nervous glimmer passing over her features.

Hesitantly, she followed Kade out of his study and stood in the doorway. She watched as he opened the front door. Kade's eyes narrowed slightly when he realized who their morning visitor was. Lord Nero stood in front of him, a smirk apparent on his lips. Kade watched the cruel man's hungry gaze as it traveled over his shoulder and fell on Morgana, who had come up behind him. He felt her place a small hand on his back, allowing him to shield her from Lord Nero's ire.

"Well, going to invite me in, doctor?" Lord Nero sneered.

"Of course. Come on in, Lord Nero."

Begrudgingly, Kade moved aside so that the man could come in the door. Lord Nero's black eyes searched around his home for a moment before settling back on Morgana. For some reason, Kade could never get used to Lord Nero's appearance and even just looking at the man unsettled him. For one thing, he was large, even by Kade's standards. He wore no shirt, but that only seemed to emphasize the rippling muscles of his chest and the baldness of his head. Black tribal tattoos snaked around every inch of bare skin, giving him an incredibly ominous appearance. Heavy gold hoops lined the man's entire ear, while a thin gold chain connected to a large golden stud in his nose.

But regardless of his appearance, the thing itching at

Kade's consciousness the most was the hungry look on Lord Nero's face as he gazed upon Morgana. It was almost as though he wanted to take her right there, in the entrance to his home.

Looking back at Morgana, he saw her steel herself. He saw the look of angry confidence come back into her eyes, replacing the momentary fear he had seen when Lord Nero had first arrived. Her violet eyes sparkled with her tenacity, and a fire like he had never seen before flared to life. It was a wonder to see.

"For what reason have we been honored by your visit, Lord Nero?" Kade said, breaking the tense silence, still using his body to separate the two.

"I thought I'd pay a visit, see how our little prisoner is getting along with one of my prized doctors. I assume you've given her a full examination?" Lord Nero said, his voice invoking something deep in Kade, something primal that he could only identify as anger and jealousy intertwined. This man had no right. Absolutely none.

Kade took a deep breath, remembering his position. Lord Nero was the leader of D'Lormere. He had to bide his time before everything he had planned would come to fruition.

"She is healthy enough. A tad on the skinny side, but I plan to fix that with healthy meals. Another few pounds and she will be as strong as ever."

"And her breeding capabilities?" Lord Nero asked, his eyes dropping suggestively to what lay between Morgana's legs. Kade saw her shiver in disgust before he answered.

"I see no reason why she could not bear children. She is sexually responsive, and has hips that would do well during childbirth."

A sickening smile came over Lord Nero's lips and it chilled Kade to the bone.

"What do you think, Morgana? Would you like to lie with the last Soul Eater on the planet? Would you like to carry my children?"

Kade stepped forward, cutting off Morgana as she began to speak, her anger clear in her voice.

"Lord Nero, I recall that you wanted me to pass on my bloodline. I have already laid my claim on this woman. She submits to me."

"She does, huh? Now that, I would like to see."

Kade took a deep breath and turned toward her. He met her eyes, imploring her to submit to him, for her own good. She watched him quizzically, almost like an animal startled by a bright light in the road. Moving closer to her, he grazed his fingers across her shoulders, tracing the smooth skin of her neck, and then he forcefully gripped a handful of her gorgeous red locks in his fist. Her mouth opened as a soft sigh left her lips. Her eyes fluttered, and he could see in them her wariness fighting the desire that threatened to come to the surface.

"Kneel."

For a moment, she hesitated, her eyes moving from his to Lord Nero behind him. He tugged her hair roughly to turn her attention back to him. Almost imperceptibly, she nodded to him and began slowly to drop to her knees. Kade allowed himself to smile softly, knowing Lord Nero couldn't see his face, and he released his hold on her hair so that she could kneel before him.

"I want you to kiss the hand that punished you yesterday, the hand that spanked your bottom so hard that it matched the pretty red hair on your head. When you are finished doing that, I want you to thank me for putting you over my knee, baring your bottom, and spanking you in order to teach you to behave."

Her lower lip pouted almost immediately in response before she caught herself. Her expression calmed, but her eyes shot daggers at him. He knew her inner turmoil, how she hated the fact that he told her greatest enemy that he had punished her like a child. Unfortunately, this was necessary. Kade knew that unless he marked Morgana as his own, Lord Nero would take her from him. He could not let that happen. He knew how Lord Nero treated his women, and in no way would he let his little sorceress fall victim to his evil clutches.

After a long moment, something changed in her eyes, and her fingers moved to cup his right hand. She turned his palm over and brought her lips to it, placing a soft kiss that ignited a fire that raged underneath his skin.

His heart pounded as she began to speak. He felt his cock stiffen at her submissive posture as she pulled her soft lips away from him.

"Thank you, sir, for putting me over your knee, baring my bottom, and spanking me until I learned the error of my ways. I am yours to do with whatever you wish, sir."

Visions of her naked bottom dancing under his punishing palm came to mind. He knew how much she had enjoyed submitting to him; her body had told him exactly how much. His cock felt impossibly tight under the constraints of his pants. Morgana lowered her eyes, and Kade turned back to Lord Nero.

"Lord Nero, with all due respect, I claim this woman as mine. I will breed her and pass on my bloodline, just as you wished for me to do."

"It is my great joy to see such a wild woman submit to you, doctor. Once a great sorceress of Legeari, and now, a simple woman put over a D'Lormerean man's knee and spanked. Keep up the good work. I expected no less from you." The smile that followed made Kade feel sick, knowing exactly what the man was imagining.

Kade glanced back at Morgana, still kneeling on the floor, and watched her little hands clench into tight fists. Quickly, he placed a hand on her head in order to stop her from doing or saying anything. Thankfully, it worked, and she didn't utter a sound.

"She's a feisty one, my lord, but I'm sure some more quality time over my knee will teach her to be a good girl."

"Be sure to take her to the punishment block and show her what happens to naughty wives here in Drentine."

"Of course."

"I could enter her into today's schedule, if you like."

"No, not quite yet. I will show her what her naughty behavior could result in. I'm sure after she sees some of the women paddled for their wrongdoings, she will think twice before she misbehaves."

"Good. If you deem punishment necessary, I will most certainly be in attendance."

"Thank you, Lord Nero. I will let you know if I require it." Kade forced himself to smile despite his simmering anger.

"I expect updates on this one. I will be watching closely to make sure you can manage her; if not, I will take her for myself."

"My lord, I would expect no less. You can trust that you have put her in good hands."

Lord Nero nodded, his features dangerously glinting in Morgana's direction before he turned away.

"I must take my leave now. See to it that she is pregnant soon."

Kade nodded his agreement before Lord Nero opened his front door and left. For a long moment, neither of them breathed as they listened for sounds of the evil man's departure. Finally, after what seemed like forever, Morgana rose to her feet and glared back at him.

"How dare you…!"

CHAPTER FOUR

Morgana stomped her foot and crossed her arms. She couldn't believe he had told Lord Nero that she had been spanked like a naughty little girl, and it was even worse that he made her say the words herself. Her face flushed, her embarrassment effectively took over her thoughts. Kade essentially cut her off by pulling her small body into her arms.

"You were wonderful!"

"I was?" she whispered, clearly confused. Her annoyance with him slowly simmered to a small flame, quickly extinguished by the look of pride that came over him.

"You submitted to me without question. Had you not, Lord Nero would have dragged you out of my home and into his. And who knows what would have happened to you then. You're safe with me, Morgana, you must see that now."

Quietly, she appraised him, narrowing her eyes slightly as she nibbled her lip. His hand cupped her face and then his thumb brushed across her mouth, blazing a line of fire straight to her core. Pushing her thighs together, she tried to ignore the telltale feeling of her arousal dampening her folds.

Kade's yellow eyes flashed as he watched her, clearly feeling as she did.

"That's why you did what you did? To protect me?"

"Yes. It makes me very happy to protect you. And even though it was terribly embarrassing for you…" He paused, his hand drifting down her torso until he stopped on her thighs. She quivered at his touch and he smiled. He cupped her sex, the silky folds of her dress caressing her aching flesh. "You loved every single second of it."

"No, I didn't!" she protested, barely repressing a moan as her body betrayed her.

"Liars get put over my knee and spanked, young lady."

Morgana lifted her chin in mock defiance. She should be angry with him; she should hate the fact he was threatening her with such a silly punishment, especially one that hurt as much as it did the day before. But, for some strange reason, her body was throbbing, every heartbeat pushing the blood through her body, making her skin impossibly hotter. The look on Kade's face was one of sheer dominance. He held her pussy in his hands like he owned it, his face stern as his threats of a spanking lingered in the air. Her bottom tingled at the thought and her pulse quickened. Morgana swallowed deeply as her mouth opened and uttered her challenge.

"Then you best teach me not to lie, sir."

She stood tall and arched her back, making sure he could see her defiance. Meeting his eyes, she saw a hint of a smile glimmer at the edge of his lips before it disappeared and was replaced by something decidedly more alpha male. His entire face took on a stern hardness as he tightened his hold on her pussy, making her excruciatingly aware of his commanding presence. Surprising even herself, she realized she wanted more.

She had never known that her body could feel this good, that she even wanted a man to command her body the way Kade did. Every time he touched her, her legs felt like jelly and desire coursed through her veins.

"Ask me."

"Ask you what?"

"Ask me to spank you."

Morgana's knees shook. She felt her wetness as it dripped from her and she knew he could feel all of it. She moaned when his fingers began to move as her pussy throbbed with need, his touch on her lower lips inciting a desperation within her that was suddenly very hard to contain. She wanted him, needed him, and this fueled her impulsive courage.

"Please, sir. Will you please spank me for lying to you? It was a terribly naughty thing to do," she managed to say, her voice wavering with trepidation and desire.

"Well, Morgana, lying is a dreadful thing. I want you to turn around and bare your backside to me. Then, I want you to walk down the hallway and wait for me in my bedroom. Bend over the bed, so that your backside is facing the door."

Her stomach dropped at his command, but she felt wetness pool even more between her thighs. He let go of her pussy, and she was almost sad until she saw the look of hunger in his eyes. He wanted her too.

Slowly, she turned around, so that he faced her back. Fumbling behind her, she found the strings that held the back of the human slave uniform together, and untied them, Pulling the fabric aside, she felt the cool air caress her naked skin. Having him bare her was certainly one thing, but being made to show him her backside, to present it to him for correction was something else entirely. Still, her body grew impossibly hotter and the throbbing between her legs was becoming the only thing she could think about.

He could see her bare bottom, every square inch of it. Soon, she would be lying over his lap, and her waiting cheeks would be feeling the effects of his palm, spanking her over and over. Her thighs began to visibly tremble and she put her hands on them to steady herself.

When she finally felt her legs regain some strength, she began to hesitantly move down the hallway. Every single step incited the throbbing between her legs, her arousal slickening her nether lips. As she made her way to his bedroom, she couldn't help but softly moan at the feeling of her folds rubbing together.

Seeing his bed, she gratefully bent over it, noticing it was the perfect height so that her upper body was fully supported, but her toes just grazed the floor. It left her feeling a little bit helpless, but in the most delicious way possible.

Shivering, she heard Kade's footsteps coming down the hallway. She knew that he could see everything: her entire bottom and the secrets between her legs. Even though he had already seen so much of her when he examined her, she still felt shy about it. It was incredibly arousing at the same time.

His masterful domination of her body was something new, but altogether wonderful. And she wanted more of it.

Her breathing quickened the closer his footsteps came to the room, until she realized he had stopped in the doorframe. She went to push herself up, but his voice commanded her attention.

"Stay still. I am admiring how pale your bottom is, so that I can remember that when I paint it the same color as your red hair."

A shiver raced down her spine, and she did her best to stay still, keeping her eyes on the soft quilt on the bed.

"Spread your legs."

Knowing exactly what he would see, she whined but did as she was told. Her back arched a little in the process, showcasing all her secrets to him with but a single movement. She felt him move up behind her, the floor creaking under his feet. Nervous excitement cascaded through her and a million questions swirled around in her head. Would the spanking hurt? Would he touch her there afterwards? Would he allow the release she was already so desperate for?

Jumping at a sudden touch, she felt his fingers lightly

trace across the backs of her thighs up toward her pussy, which was already glistening with her arousal. Knowing he had knelt behind her, her hips rolled as she tried to keep still. He could see everything. And he could most certainly see how wild with desire he was making her.

The sensation of being examined so intimately nearly undid her. He kissed the tops of her legs, the sensitive area at the crease where her thighs met her bottom, and she arched her back even harder. His kisses there felt delicious, shooting flares of desire straight to her core. Finally, he placed a kiss straight on the folds of her pussy, his tongue inching up to caress her pulsating clit. Arching into him, her moans become increasingly frantic.

She didn't think she could take much more of this. Her nipples were so hard that they hurt.

She felt his presence as he stood beside her, then sat down on the bed. As he pulled her over his lap, she suddenly felt nervous. Her bottom was terribly exposed, waiting for him to spank it. A soft whine escaped her throat.

His fingers grazed her sensitive skin, and she melted into him, rolling her hips against his rock-solid thigh. She could feel his hardness underneath her, and she felt a little apprehensive when she realized just how big it was.

Her bottom tingled as he lifted his hand and brought it back down to smack her quivering globes. Quickly, he brought his hand back down on the opposite side. It took a long moment for the sting to reach Morgana's head, so wild with desire she felt. The sound echoed throughout the room, so much more terrible than the slight sting that registered within her. He spanked her again and again, all the while sliding his fingers between her legs and brushing against her very slick folds. Before long, she was shamelessly rolling her hips against him in wild abandon, arching her back to meet his spanks, and trying to prolong his touches to her ever willing pussy.

"Spread your legs."

Quickly she obeyed, panting so hard she could hardly

stand it.

"Tell me, Morgana, were you a naughty girl? Do you deserve to be punished?"

"Yes, sir. Please, I was very naughty. Please punish me," she whimpered, hopelessly grinding against him, her legs wantonly spread. She almost couldn't believe the words coming out of her mouth.

Kade placed his palm against her pussy, sliding his fingers between her very wet lips.

"Naughty girls get their pussy spanked."

Lifting his hand, he brought it back down on her moist folds. The sound of his palm clapping against her wetness made her blush instantly, until she was assaulted with an intense sensation that blended pleasure with a hint of pain. He brought his palm down again and again against her pussy, and she cried out at how much her body responded.

Morgana lost count how many times he spanked her pussy, because she was soon lost as she toppled over the edge into one of the most intense orgasms she had ever had in her life. Her moans echoed throughout the room, only slightly louder than his smacks on her glistening wet flesh.

Wildly, she ground against him, and his fingers found her throbbing bud, circling it, kneading it. Clinging to him, she rode his hand, her legs shamelessly spread as he explored everything between them. He kept a steady pressure on her clit as she finished experiencing one orgasm, and then rapidly built into a second one. His other hand grabbed her hip, holding her firm over his thigh, as he wrung more pleasure out of her than she ever thought possible.

When her orgasm finally faded, she lay spent over his knees. Kade spanked her bottom, once on each side, hard enough to cause her to mewl in protest.

Honestly, it didn't hurt though; it just emphasized the feelings of lust hurtling throughout her system. Tremors continually shook her for several moments before Kade picked her up and hugged her to his chest. Her bare bottom and throbbing pussy were pressed against his hard thigh. She held onto him for support, her body weak from the powerful assault of pleasure that had just taken over her.

He grabbed a fistful of her hair and pulled her head back so that he could meet her eyes.

"You, my naughty sorceress, enjoy submitting to me."

"Yes, sir," she whispered, her voice hoarse from her moans. The fingers from his other hand snaked up her thigh, before he paused at the opening of her slick channel.

"Beg for it."

Morgana felt her hips move toward him, whimpering when she realized how empty she felt. She tried to adjust herself so that he had to press his fingers deep inside her.

"Morgana…" he warned.

"Please, sir. Please fuck me with your fingers."

"Good girl."

Not a moment later, she felt his two large fingers enter her, sliding in easily with her aroused state. Before long, she had her hands on his shoulders and she was riding his fingers. Without a care in the world, she came again, shuddering into his touch, holding him as she frantically ground into him, her pussy clenching around him. As quickly as he brought her to another orgasm, it took forever for her to come back down to real life again. Breathing hard, she clutched him close, and he held her.

He brushed her wild hair out of her face and she looked shyly back at him, hyperaware of her behavior at his hands. She felt flushed and her heart continued to pound in her chest, until that too gradually calmed to a gentle beat.

Predatory eyes looked back at her, his yellow eyes still hungry for her. She shrank back, suddenly a little wary of him. His eyes softened upon observing her reaction.

"Morgana, do you fear me?"

"I don't know much about you, other than the fact that you can drive me completely insane with what you do to me. I know you're some sort of Erassan, but I don't know any more than that. I don't really know anything about you."

"My favorite color is red," he replied with a small smirk.

Morgana giggled at the ridiculousness of his response.

"I can tell you my favorite food, or my favorite dream vacation, or even my favorite animal, but you have to promise to keep it secret, keep it safe. It's classified information," he continued, beginning to tickle her. Laughing even harder, she pulled away and tried to catch her breath, and he began again.

"But in all seriousness, I want to take you to meet the rest of my bloodline. Granted, my father was killed and my mother disappeared, but I have been able to find many of my other family relatives. I wanted to introduce you to them."

"Will I find out why Lord Nero is so obsessed with breeding you with me?"

"You will. But I want to show you something first."

Kade helped her to climb off his lap and onto the bed. He stood in front of her and began to disrobe, taking off his shirt first.

"What are you doing?" she asked, suddenly nervous.

"I've destroyed too many sets of clothes in the changing process that now, I just get naked first."

"Oh," she replied with a nervous giggle. What did he mean by changing process?

Kade took off his shoes and socks, and then pulled off his pants, leaving everything neatly on a nearby chair. He stood in front of her in just a pair of black boxers. Her mouth opened in shock and blatant admiration of his male form. Gasping, she took in the sight.

She had never been so affected by a man's physique before in her life. His chest muscles were remarkably cut, leading down to a stomach rippling with his movements. His corded biceps and strong shoulders moved to a muscled chest, tapering down to a narrow waist. His hip bones cast an alluring 'v' shape, causing her to stare down even lower. With a heavy swallow, she followed the trail of hair from his belly button down to the top of his underwear. She saw the shape of his member through the fabric, straining to be released. All of a sudden, she wanted to see it, in all of its glory. Raising her eyes to meet his, she waited for him to get rid of the last piece of clothing on his body.

She was not disappointed.

Kade gripped the waistband of his boxers and slid them down his large muscled thighs. Time seemed to slow as he placed them on the chair with the rest of his clothes. Her eyes tore back to his cock, and she found that she couldn't look away.

His cock was massive. It was long and thick, and it was remarkably hard. Swallowing deeply, she wondered if it would even fit inside her. Licking her lips, she was finally able to look away and back up at his eyes. He was smiling, but didn't say a word about her lingering gaze.

"I'm a special kind of Erassan, Morgana. My bloodline has a very rare ability that we have been careful to pass on generation after generation. I'm a shifter. I have the capability to turn into my wolf form at will."

"A wolf shifter?"

"Yes. Now, do not be afraid. I have full control of everything I do, even in my animal form."

Morgana watched as he took a step back from her. Curling her legs up into her chest, she waited and watched as a calm look of concentration came over him.

His whole physique began to change. First, his head arched backwards and his body rounded, his hands coming into contact with the floor. His body seemed to grow impossibly larger, dark fur suddenly becoming visible all over his body. His fingers spread out wide before they took on the shape of very large paws. Finally, after what seemed like ages later, a massive black wolf stood in front of her. Yellow irises stared back at her; still strangely warm and familiar as he gazed into her eyes.

Morgana had seen large wolves before, like Tala, the king's steed, but she could have sworn she had never seen anything larger than him in her life. Pushing herself off the bed, she stood in front of the massive wolf and his frame towered over her. Reaching up, she smoothed the fur behind his ear and down his neck. He was soft to the touch.

"Can you speak in my mind like the native wolves on the planet?"

"*Yes. Only my power is greater when I'm in my wolf form. If you would look in my eyes, I can show you.*"

Moving back in front of him, Morgana lifted her eyes to meet his, and felt his immense power take over her body. Unexpectedly, waves of desire crashed over her, and she barely held herself up on her feet. It was overwhelming in its sudden force and she braced herself on the bed behind her, her insides churning with lust.

"What did you do?" she asked, breathless as his power receded away.

"*I can make a person feel anything I wish the moment they meet my eyes. They can fear me, love me, want me, or anything I want them to feel.*"

"That was intense."

"*It certainly can be. Our bloodline has kept our powers secret for a long time, but Lord Nero found out my capabilities when I was taken hostage. Ever since then, he's wanted an heir so that he could use them in order to get what he wants.*"

"I'm sorry."

"*It's not your fault. I'm going to take you to meet the members of my pack. I want you to meet some of my allies that have gathered under Nero's harsh rule. You'll be surprised at just how many of us there are.*"

"Are you going to go just like that?"

A soft growl sounded in the room, rumbling the walls with its intensity. It almost sounded like he was laughing and she smiled back at him.

"You sound ferocious," she joked and watched as his wolf form began to get smaller and smaller, until once again, Kade stood in front of her in his human form.

"No. I wouldn't want to call attention to us that way. Wolf steeds are not as common here in Drentine," he replied as he pulled his clothes back on. Morgana watched him, still admiring the raw power he held, even in his human form.

"Do you know of any other Erassan shifters?"

"No, but our type tends to keep to ourselves for the most part. My pack is very selective about our choices of partners because of the importance of our secret. Lord Nero may know that I carry the power of a wolf shifter, but he doesn't know anyone else in my pack that does. And it is imperative that things stay that way."

"Based on what he wants to do with your children, I can certainly understand why."

"He's an evil man who doesn't care for his people, but spends his days trying to figure out how to heighten his own station. It doesn't matter who he destroys in that process, as long as it gets done."

Morgana stood and tied her slave garb shut, covering her backside with the sheer red fabric. She slipped her feet into small black ballet flats that she found behind the bed. When she looked back at Kade, he was already fully dressed and waiting for her. He offered her his hand and she moved forward to take it. His large hand enveloped her much smaller one and he led her out of the room.

He stopped in the kitchen and fetched a glass of water, waiting as she drank it. At first she protested, but then realized how parched her throat was, what with her loud moans from their earlier activities. Smiling softly, she whispered her thanks and handed him the empty glass.

Before she knew it, they were heading out of his house, into the light of day. Squinting, her eyes adjusted to the bright sun and she looked around. The city was bustling. Tall buildings made of glass and metal rose around them, very different from the city of Eridell where she had spent most of her time. There were no friendly faces passing smiles, or people exchanging conversation. They walked facing straight ahead, with the only thing seemingly on their minds being their destination. With a start, she realized that she didn't see a single human on the street. Every single one was an Erassan. A twinge of worry began develop deep in the pit of her stomach.

"Is it safe for me out here?"

"As long as you are escorted by your Erassan owner, yes. You are to never leave my home without me. Our laws do not protect you."

Morgana looked around, silently accepting what he had to say. Her hand drifted to her neck, to the thick leather collar that suddenly felt very heavy.

"You're not using the leash this time," she murmured quietly.

"I think you know the consequences of trying to run from me, don't you?"

She made a face at him as a blush crept up her face. Embarrassed, she most certainly knew what he would do. He would spank her and there was nothing she could do about it. Her bottom cheeks tingled in anticipation and she looked away. Reluctantly, she opened her mouth to answer him.

"Yes, sir. I certainly do…"

"Come, we need to catch a travel ship. Those of my bloodline do not dare to live in the city. The ship will take us to the edge of the city, but we will have to walk some ways on foot to reach our camp."

"That far away?"

"Yes. We have to keep our women and children safe."

"Have you always known about your pack?"

"No; not long ago, one of them arrived at my door. He had felt drawn to a presence in the city and then he found me. Their pack had been without an alpha male for some time, and when he sensed me, he knew he had finally found what he was looking for. I went to visit the pack, and they accepted me as their alpha. Their blood demanded it and my blood rose to the challenge."

Kade stepped forward and waved down a small air ship, big enough for the driver and the two of them. It whizzed down and stopped in front of them. Admiring its smooth steel hull, she noticed some strange sort of writing on the side. Upon further inspection, she recognized it for native D'Lormerean. Kade opened the passenger door and helped her inside. She sat down on the black leather bench seat at the back of the cabin, and he climbed inside after her.

"Take us to the factory district. Warehouse 72."

The driver looked back and nodded his head. Morgana kept her questions to herself for the time being. She had faith that Kade would explain things to her when they arrived. Instead, she leaned back into the seat and relaxed against his large body. He seemed to emanate a heat warmer than no other, which kept her slightly chilled self from getting too cold. She looked out the tiny side window, observing the wide variety of tall buildings, and gray stone roads that Erassans walked on down below. As they flew through the city, she marveled by how large it was. Off in the distance, she could see a massive wall that enclosed the area, keeping the inhabitants inside and others out. The closer they got to the wall, the more nervous she became.

Didn't Kade say that they had to travel outside the city to get to his pack's camp? The wall was gigantic, even more so than the one that surrounded the city of Eridell. It was so high that it towered over many of the tallest buildings that were a part of Drentine.

The capital of D'Lormere was nothing like she ever imagined, and the more she saw of it, the more she worried about the fate of her home, Legeari. Would King Dante ever prevail over the evils of Lord Nero?

The trip to the city wall passed by quickly, as lost in her thoughts as she was. While her worries tumbled around in her head, she allowed Kade to assist her out of the small travel ship. He waited until the craft had flown some ways away before turning back to her.

"The factory district is not very well patrolled. It is also one of the weakest points in the wall. There is a drainage point not far from here that is no longer used, and allows members of my pack to come and go as they please, as long as they are careful."

He looked around and began walking behind a large factory building. The wall rose before her, imposing in its design. Large gray stones laid in row after row, rising far overhead. It felt much like a prison to her.

"Can citizens not leave the city of Drentine?"

"There is an exit in the market district, but an individual has to receive special permission in order to leave the city, or enter it, for that matter."

"And I imagine it is difficult to obtain such a privilege."

"It's becoming increasingly challenging the longer Lord Nero leads our people," he said, his face taking on a calm grimness like she hadn't seen before. "There's a lot of unhappiness with his rule, and whispers of an uprising have been becoming more common. People are beginning to get restless."

She placed one hand on the cool stone and gazed back at him.

"If that happens and Lord Nero hears of it, a lot of people are going to die."

"I know. Each and every day, it gets more and more dangerous to be here."

Finally, he stopped in front of a deteriorating piece of the wall, hidden well behind the factory building. Pushing aside some debris, he uncovered a grate that he quickly moved aside.

"I'll help you climb down. Trust me, it's only a short way down, but it's very dark," he said, as he held out his hand to her. Hesitantly, she took it, and he led her to a rope ladder she hadn't seen at first. Carefully, he helped her make the short climb to the ground. Glancing around, her eyes gradually adjusted to the dim lighting. She moved aside as he made his way down the ladder till he was standing beside her.

For a moment, she had admired how his pants conformed to the outline of his buttocks, to the lean muscle in his thighs, and she felt her heart begin to beat just a little bit faster. Looking away, she didn't meet his eyes as he turned toward her, and instead looked around the damp path. A shiver raced up her spine at the dark vegetation growing on the stone and the constant drip of water coming from somewhere close by chilled her to the bone.

It certainly wasn't the most glamorous way to travel.

Kade took her hand and they began to venture into the enclosed space. Thankfully, the path wasn't very long, and they were on the other side before she knew it. Looking back, the tall wall was thick, but not impossibly so. She would have to take note of this weak spot in the wall, in case the information could be useful for King Dante.

Making sure to avoid a few puddles forming on the stones, she followed Kade to another rope ladder on the other side. He ushered her to ascend first and she climbed the ladder, glancing back to see him admiring her rear end, just as she had his.

Concentrating on pulling herself up onto the soft grass outside the wall, she smiled to herself. Maybe, just maybe, he was attracted to her too.

By the time he was standing next to her, she was looking out at the vast forest beyond the wall. Massive trees rose well over her head, their leaves green and their branches full. She couldn't see much other than a wall of wide trunks in any direction. There was a certain ominous presence here, almost as though there were plenty of dark hidden secrets contained in the depths of the jungle before her.

"We're going in there?" she asked, her voice coming across much apprehensive than she had intended.

"Yes. Don't worry, I'll be right by your side. Come, it'll be faster if you ride on my back when I'm in my wolf form."

She nodded, watching as he undressed before her. Folding his clothes and leaving them in a pile behind a tree, he stood before her, naked. Not being able to get used to the sight, her eyes studied his body, trying to memorize the muscles in his chest, his sculpted abs, and especially the girth of his cock. With a heavy swallow, she jumped as she realized that he was fully aware of her wandering eyes. Looking away as a flush crept up her face, she finally looked back after a few long moments.

The massive black wolf with Kade's yellow eyes was staring back at her. They studied her with such intensity that she almost took a step backwards. Instead, she forced herself to walk toward him, and placed a hand on his shoulder. He knelt down and she was able to climb atop him with ease. Straddling his back, she took a hold of some of the long fur on the back of his neck.

"Is this alright? That doesn't hurt, right?"

Something that sounded like half growl, half laugh emerged from the wolf's mouth. With a soft headshake, Kade took off into the woods. Giggling softly, Morgana realized her question was probably a very silly one.

He glided through the woods, twisting and turning on some unseen path, at least to her. He was so majestic in his movements that for much of the time, she ignored the feeling of the wind whipping through her hair, and instead focused on the raw power encased within the animal she sat astride. Each bound he took as he ran covered an impossibly large distance, each step sound and sure. Even though he hadn't said a word, a quiet confidence seemed to roll off him in waves.

He was nothing short of beautiful. His black fur shone, luminescent in the soft sunlight that managed to make its way to the forest floor. Bending forward, she looped her arms around his neck, allowing her entire body to feel his every moment. It was an intoxicating experience.

The two of them traveled this way for well over an hour, escaping deeper and deeper into the depths of the mysterious jungle. Finally, the trees opened up to a soft meadow, and a short distance away, a large lake lapped at its edges. Hidden in the trees, Morgana saw a few rural cottages built into the shadows. The more she concentrated, the more she saw. There was an entire village concealed here, deep in the woods, free from Lord Nero's clutches.

"Is this your pack, Kade?"

"*Yes. Welcome to my family. There have been whispers of our existence throughout time here on Terranovum. They call us the Lost Shadows of the Dark Forest in the myths I've seen but we like to call ourselves the Pack of the Blood Rose.*"

"Pack of the Blood Rose? What's the meaning behind that?"

"*Our females are very important to us. We are one of the few species of Erassans that can give birth to a viable female, and for her to have the capability to have children herself. As you know well, that is not the case for the majority of them, as their women are mainly infertile. They need human women in order to produce children that can procreate. We've kept this secret for millennia. Our women are like precious roses to us, and we are willing to spill our blood in order to protect them.*"

"That's amazing. They can have children? Without breeding human women?"

"*We don't quite know why. We just know that it's a secret that is worth protecting with our lives. Our women are sacred to us.*"

Morgana bit her lip, wondering if he had a woman back here, an Erassan woman, someone worthy of his status of alpha. She hoped he didn't. He was their alpha male. In all likelihood, he probably had a wife, or was at least promised to a high-ranking female within his pack. Why would he want a human female like her when he could have whomever he wanted?

Glancing down at the wretched bracelet hanging around her wrist, she remembered that right now, she was a simple human. That was it. For several years, her magic had been a very big part of her. Ever since Lord Nero had stolen it from her, she had felt empty, and even a little bit lonely. She felt a little bit like her fire was diminished.

Looking back at Kade, still in his massive wolf form, she smiled slightly. Even if he had a woman already, at least she could consider him a friend. He hadn't given her a single reason not to trust him yet, but still, she should be a little wary of him. He could be trying to gain her loyalty, just to betray her to Lord Nero. She'd have to be very careful with what she told him, even though she was beginning to really like him.

Admonishing herself, she thought about Eridell and her king. She had been only eighteen when she was taken from Earth. In retrospect, it was a blessing in disguise and now, she didn't regret being taken for a single moment.

She remembered the night she was taken in vivid detail, and allowed the memory to take over her thoughts.

Her day had been miserable. She hadn't eaten since the day before, and wasn't able to scrounge up enough money for something off the dollar menu at the local fast food restaurants. The sun was beginning to drop, and she realized she would probably go hungry for the night. Placing her hand on her stomach, she willed the hurt to go away, telling herself that she wasn't hungry, that she would be fine if she waited until tomorrow.

Needing to get her mind off her rumbling stomach, she wandered down the boardwalk and onto the beach. Atlantic City was dead this time of year, the early spring winds scaring the tourists away. Pulling off her socks and sneakers, she let the soft cold sand surround her toes. Relishing the residual warmth of the sun, she meandered further down the beach to where the tide was just beginning to come in. The water barely touched her skin, causing a shiver to race up her spine. Pushing back a little away from the ocean, she sat down on the sand and hugged her knees to her chest.

Alone. That's how she had felt for weeks. None of her relatives had wanted to care for her, not wanting an unruly teenager in their houses. She hadn't been the most well-behaved child; usually apt to speak her mind no matter the trouble it caused her. She had been left to her own devices, forgotten by whatever welfare administration agency that was supposed to be watching out for her. Having been forced to grow up fast, she had been caring for herself ever since.

She missed her parents. Ever since they had passed, her life had been hell, trying to find a meal for the day and a warm place to sleep. The homeless shelters were filling up faster by the day, and often, by the time they got to her place in line, there was no longer any space for her. Tonight hadn't been any different. Making the decision to try to raise enough money for dinner had taken precedence, and she had made the executive decision that food was more important than shelter tonight. Unfortunately, she had only raised about twenty-five cents. So because of her bad decision, she was going to go hungry and cold until morning.

A tear rolled down her cheek as she looked out at the ocean. She swiped it away with the back of her hand, smearing dirt on her face in the process. If only she could at least take a shower, and clean herself of the grime of the city.

Hiding her face in her hands, sobs wracked her body. Hopelessness washed over her. What would she do? How could she continue to live like this?

"I can make it all better, if you but give me a chance," a soft, but commanding voice sounded near her. Normally, such a thing would have put her off, but there was something about his tone, something that told her he wasn't looking for sex.

Uncovering her eyes, each finger dropping slowly to look at the man kneeling in front of her, she gasped at the sight. Ice blue eyes stared back at her, and when she gazed back at him, suddenly all her feelings of sadness melted away. All that was left was an incredible sense of warmth and safety.

Messy dark hair framed a strong, but stern face. There was a soft hint of dark stubble surrounding his chin, and a kind smile glimmered at the edges of his lips. His shoulders were wide, accented by rippling muscles that she could discern under his dark t-shirt.

"My name is Dante."

"I'm Morgana," she paused, before continuing. "You won't hurt me?" she whimpered, not knowing if she could handle any more misery this day.

He leaned forward and his hand brushed a piece of her unruly red hair out of her face. She almost melted into the man's touch before remembering herself.

"No. I won't hurt you. But I will give you a choice. You can come with me to my home, and be granted a whole new life. You will eat every day and have a safe place to sleep. But the catch is that you must obey every command that is given to you, no matter what it is."

Curling her arms around herself, she gazed back at this man, this Dante, and wondered what he meant.

"Come with you, and obey you?"

"You will be safe. No one would be allowed to hurt you ever again."

"You won't force yourself on me?"

"No," he responded, his voice turning deadly serious. "That is strictly forbidden in my kingdom." She watched his icy blue eyes for a moment, seeing flames of red begin to lick around the edges of his irises. What was he? Was he human?

He held out his hand and she stared at it. What should she do?

"I can promise you a better life than this. I will personally make sure that you are well taken care of in the castle."

He seemed to be talking nonsense; a castle? His kingdom? But, to be honest, it didn't seem to matter to her. His hand was still outstretched, begging her to take it, to take a chance. She met his eyes once again and he nodded, encouraging her.

Hesitantly, she reached out her own hand, pausing before she touched his. With a swallow, she pushed her hand forward, her cold skin brushing against his warmth. Slowly, he helped her to stand and his other hand cupped her chin, forcing her eyes to stay on his.

"Trust me."

As she looked into his soft blue eyes, her world began to spin and her body felt like it was falling. She noticed that his grip tightened, holding her firm against his body as her world went black. That night, she knew no more.

The next time she opened her eyes, she was on planet Terranovum, in the capital city of Legeari, Eridell. She was brought to the bathhouses, cleaned thoroughly, and fed a rather large meal. Having eaten every bite, she was then taken back to Dante's quarters. It wasn't until later that she had found out that he was king.

She climbed into the large bed and promptly fell back to sleep, exhaustion quickly catching up with her. Feeling movement on the bed some time later, she slowly opened her eyes to see Dante sitting before her.

He was openly staring at her.

"What? Do I have something in my teeth?" she asked, a little

groggily.

Instead, he took her hand and lifted it into her view. Confused, she watched him before her eyes flickered down to look at her wrist.

It was glowing. Light seemed to emanate from her every pore, every color of the rainbow seemingly drifted across her skin. Sitting up straight in bed, her other hand came around to touch herself, to feel the warmth of the light coming from her.

"What is happening to me?"

"You have the gift of magic, my little human. You are a sorceress."

The rest of that day had been a blur. She had been taken to the Hall of Magic and tested for her abilities. It was decided that she had the strongest power for a human seen in several hundred years, and as a result, she was assigned to protect the king. Ever since that moment, she had been pampered and taken care of. Dante had kept his word, and seen to it that she had everything that she could have ever wanted. She had seen his goodness, hidden under the grief of loss he carried around like his own personal cross. She knew he had a good heart, and that he cared for his people with a fervor like she had never seen before. No matter the decisions he had to make, whether they be popular or not, he made them with his people at the forefront of his mind. He was the true meaning of a king in her eyes.

They had spent most days together ever since, her learning to use her magic, him asking her for her opinion on a variety of matters from war, to politics, to the welfare of his people. They had grown very close over the years she had been under his care. She knew, without a doubt, that she would be loyal to her king until she drew her last breath.

A sound in the distance jostled her thoughts, bringing her back to the clearing in the forest with Kade by her side. Blinking her memories away, she glanced toward the sound, and nearly took a step back.

A line of massive wolves was coming her way. There were at least ten of them, of all shades and colors, from grays, to browns, to coppery reds and white. There were no other black wolves, Kade's coat unique in its own right. Standing closer to him, she watched as a number of suspicious yellow eyes trained on her, and then glided over to Kade standing beside her.

She vowed not to be afraid; instead she stood tall and remembered her position. She was Morgana, the king's sorceress, and a force to be reckoned with. In her days serving Dante, she had faced much worse. Even if she didn't have her magic, she couldn't allow herself to be weak in anyone else's eyes.

The pack of wolves stopped about six feet away from her, staring at the two of them. Morgana was so engrossed in the eyes of the big wolves that she hardly noticed when a group of woman and children came up behind the wolves. She stepped forward, her confidence beginning to grow once again.

"My name is Morgana, and I am King Dante's sorceress. I am pleased to meet all of you. Kade has told me some of the history involving your pack. Thank you for meeting me in light of the dangers involved for all of you."

She stood silently, appraising the group for another moment. Then, all the wolves began to shift back to their human form. Having already seen Kade shift from human to wolf and back, she watched in fascination as the line of wolves transformed into tall, excruciatingly handsome men, each tempting in their own right. Every one of them was naked, and Morgana did her best to keep her eyes on their fierce-looking gazes. The women came up behind them, each handing one of the men a pair of dark pants.

A blond woman walked up to them, approaching Kade. It was only then that Morgana realized that Kade had shifted as well. He took the pair of jeans from the woman with a smile before pulling them on, covering his naked body as well. Before long, the group was fully human, but still incredibly alluring. Muscled chests still rippled under the light of the sun, as the group moved in closer toward Kade and Morgana.

"It is good to see you all again. I bring before you Morgana, the woman I believe is the key to our success in our efforts against Lord Nero and his evil. She is capable of great power; enough that Lord Nero gave her to me, so that I may breed her for his purposes. Little does he know, I have no intention of giving him anything he wants. In fact, I intend to take everything away from him. It has been prophesied that the wolves that live in shadow would one day come upon a power great enough to bathe them once again in the light of the sun, and I believe Morgana is that power."

Kade's voice rang out, clear and confident in the meadow, and all eyes were attuned to him. Looks of respect passed through the crowd, and she saw a few nods here and there.

Another man stepped forward in the crowd, his dark hair speckled with gray. His body still spoke of its past youth, the muscles strong and firm as he walked. Gray stubble peppered the older man's face.

"How do we know she can be trusted?" the man's gruff voice sounded in return.

"She wants to take Lord Nero down as much as I do. And anyone who wants to destroy him that much is trustworthy in my book. I ask that you respect my decision to bring her here and show her kindness. With her input, I want to begin putting some of our plans into place."

The older man nodded, trusting Kade's word, and walked up to Morgana. He extended his hand, allowing her to take it.

"It's a pleasure to meet you, Morgana. My name is Max."

"It's nice to meet you, Max." She shook his hand before stepping back and looking at Kade, searching for an indication of what should be done next. He proceeded to introduce her to most of the members of the pack. Being as polite as she could, she tried to remember most of the names he pointed out to her, but to no avail. In the end, she could only remember Max's name, and the name of the pretty blonde she had seen giving Kade the pair of jeans. Her name was Tina. Every face was extraordinarily friendly, as though they trusted Kade's every word without a shadow of a doubt. He was truly their alpha in every way. They followed his lead, welcoming her into their ranks just because he told them to. It was fascinating to watch.

Morgana was given the grand tour. Hidden in the trees were more buildings than she thought possible. They took her into the Great Hall, and she was surprised at how many people there were. Apparently, only a small group had come to meet them on the clearing. The rest of the pack thrived in the forest, living under the shelter of the heavy trees. She was welcomed with opened arms, fed a delicious meal, and was included during some discussion on strategy. They gave her a new pair of pants, a fresh white shirt, and sturdier shoes for her feet.

All the while, she kept a suspicious watch on Tina and Kade. The blonde seemed to follow his every move, and she seemed to anticipate his every need, filling his wineglass the moment it was empty, bringing him fruit to snack on, and more food when his plate was empty. The longer that Morgana watched them interact, the more out of place she felt. Kade was friendly with her, smiling at her, touching her arm, even brushing her hair out of her face. Every time Morgana saw him touch her, she felt her heart deflate just a little bit.

By the end of the day, she was sure that they were more than friends, and she felt her blood begin to boil. Why had he touched her like he had done in his home, when he was most certainly promised to another? Even now, just the thought of the touch of his skin on her flesh made her heart pound and her thighs quiver.

As the sun set, Max and his men built a bonfire close to the lake, and everyone gathered around it. Morgana stood looking out over the water, and glanced back at the happy faces around the fire. Tina and Kade were sitting together, and his arm was around her shoulders. It seemed as though no one was paying attention to her. Her eyes shifted to the trees in the woods, and she looked back at the group.

Now was her chance. If she could slip away, she could

return to Eridell and tell the king everything she knew. She could give him their strategy, tell him about everything that was happening in Drentine, and about the growing resistance to Lord Nero's evil ways. Slowly, she turned away and began to walk to the houses in the trees. By the time she made it past a few massive trunks, she glanced backwards and not a soul had moved. Kade hadn't even noticed her absence, his booming laugh sounding in the clearing as he chatted with Tina, seemingly catching up on lost time.

Turning away, she brushed a small tear from her face. She had thought something might come of her time with Kade, but now, seeing him and Tina together, she knew she had been wrong. Allowing herself to get caught up in something like a romance was a mistake. Her duty was to her king, first and foremost. Matters of the heart were not important. They never were. She should have known better than to get caught up in this mess.

Working her way through the trees, she stopped and looked back, but the forest was silent. Continuing her journey, she made her way north, toward Eridell and her king.

CHAPTER FIVE

Kade sat next to his sister, throwing his arm around her. Tina giggled and ducked out from under him, running away with a smile on her face. It had been some time since he had seen her, and her antics were the same as ever. She was young, just barely over the age of twenty, but she had a good head on her shoulders. Her intelligence was her strength, as well as her keen eyes, which had helped to gather some critical intel on locations within Drentine. She was an asset to the pack.

Back when Lord Nero attacked his home, his sister had gone missing. He'd come to find out the little hellion had been out exploring the nearby woods when she had been explicitly told not to. When she had seen the horror that had befallen his village, she had stayed hidden. He found her years later, here in the home of his pack.

His eyes searched around for Morgana, seeking out his feisty little redhead. Standing up, the longer he looked, the more his unease grew. She was nowhere to be seen.

"Tina. Have you seen Morgana?" His voice was suddenly very serious. She looked back at him with wide eyes and shook her head. He saw her begin to scan the group as well, but she didn't come up with anything either.

Max was sitting beside them, and his face was beginning to show his concern too.

"Max. Gather up a search party. Morgana has gone missing." The man nodded, stood and went to follow orders. Within a few moments, he had gathered up a small group. Kade joined them and all the men shifted into their wolf forms.

They spread out into a search formation and entered the forest. It didn't take long for the pack to catch her scent, and they followed it for a few hours into the night. They found her before long, but Kade told the members of his pack to fall behind.

He would handle her himself, and no matter the reason, she would soon find herself bare bottomed and over his knee getting the spanking of her life for the worry she had caused him and his people.

He watched her as she was walking forward through the woods. Kade flanked her on the right side before overtaking her and making his way around in front of her. He sat a few hundred feet ahead of her, shifted into his human form, pulled on a pair of pants he had carried in his jaws, and waited for her to come to him.

A twig snapped in her direction and she walked into the small clearing where he was waiting. He leaned against a tree and watched as her form moved forward, her eyes on her feet. She hadn't seen him yet.

"Thought you could escape me that easily, huh, little dove?" he said softly, yet his voice rang out in the silence of the forest. Her head shot up to meet his eyes, and the look that crossed her face was one of anger, surprise, and a hint of bold defiance. She certainly had not expected to run into him here.

"Kade! What are you doing here?"

"You disappeared from camp, and here I find you, deep in the forest, trying to escape to Eridell by yourself. I showed you nothing but kindness, and this is how you repay me?"

"I owe you nothing. I am simply returning to my home and my people."

"I would have taken you there."

"Your place isn't with me. You and I both know that."

"Come here, Morgana." She stilled as his voice took on a very stern tone. He struggled to keep a smirk off his face as one of her hands moved backwards to shield her bottom.

"Why?" Her back arched with her rebelliousness, and she took a step back.

"You're going to get a spanking."

"No, I'm not!"

"Yes, you are. You openly defied me and left the camp, without food, or clothing, or weapons to protect you. And now I see, you are hiding something from me. By the time I paint your pretty little bottom the same color as your hair, you are going to tell me what it is."

"You're crazy! Just let me go and you could be rid of me, so I'm not in the way."

"Why would I want to be rid of you?"

She didn't answer. Instead he watched as she bolted off into the forest, and he took off after her. When he caught her, she was not only going to feel his hand on her bare bottom, but a freshly cut switch as well.

She ran swiftly, but was no match for his longer legs and greater stamina. He caught up with her in no time and grabbed her about the waist. Her legs kicked and her arms flailed, but he held her close to him as he sat down on a nearby log. He pinned her over his thighs and began to spank her clothing-covered backside.

Her yell of anger pierced through the forest. "How dare you lay a hand on me!"

"Oh, Morgana, I've barely even started!" His arms snaked around her waist and untied the drawstring of her pants. In one swift motion, he bared her bottom, revealing a thin pair of lacy white panties. They framed her heart-shaped bottom cheeks in such a way that caused his heart to quicken. He wanted to explore what was between her legs, make her quiver under his hand, and scream his name in desire and need for him. He placed his hand on her soft skin, tracing the curve of her buttocks, her skin only a very faint pink from the punishment so far. Almost with a sigh, he gripped the waistband of the panties and pushed them down her thighs.

His eyes took in her naked bottom, beautiful as it trembled in the cool air. Her quivering flesh was waiting for her punishment. She had stilled when her skin had been exposed to the fresh air, and then his fingers touched her upper thighs.

"Morgana?"

"Yes, sir?"

He smiled as he realized she had begun submitting to her punishment. Grazing his hand over her skin, he cupped her bottom right cheek.

"You're about to be punished. You were a very naughty girl, isn't that right."

"Yes, sir," she wailed, kicking her feet on the ground.

"Why did you run away? And don't you lie to me, young lady. You're already about to get the spanking you clearly deserve. Don't make it worse for yourself by lying to me."

She was quiet for a long second. Kade quickly lost his patience and spanked her left cheek followed by her right, hard. He watched as a pink handprint appeared on her pale bare skin.

"Please, sir! I saw you with her! I saw how you looked at her. How could you betray her with what you did with me? She's your beloved, not me. I'm nothing!"

Confusion grew deep in his stomach.

"Who do you mean, Morgana? Who do you think is my beloved?"

"Tina," she whispered, her voice pitiful.

"You think Tina is my beloved."

"Yes, sir…"

He laughed a little before beginning to scold the woman over his knee. Her behavior was utterly ridiculous. If only she had asked him who Tina was before, she would have saved herself the very red bottom she was about to receive.

"Morgana. I want you to listen to me right now. Then, you're going to get spanked harder than ever before for your very naughty behavior. Is that clear?"

"Yes, sir." Her voice was pitifully sad.

"Tina is my sister. Had you only asked, then you would have known and you wouldn't be here, about to get your bottom blistered for running away from me. Instead, you chose to run away, back to your kingdom instead of trusting me as you should have done."

"She's your sister? You never said you had one…"

"No, I never got the chance. When my village was attacked, my father was killed and my mother stole away, my sister had gone out into the nearby woods to go swimming in the river. They had never even known she existed. I found her here, years later. The pack, at least those that were left, had cared for her ever since."

"Oh."

"That's right. This was all a misunderstanding. You were stubborn and decided you knew the answer on your own."

"I'm sorry. I didn't know."

"This is why I'm going to spank you. Not because you didn't know, but because you ran off without asking me first. You decided that you knew the answer. Now hear this, I won't keep you as my prisoner, but if you want to leave, you must tell me why first."

"Yes, sir. I understand."

He felt her body relax over his hard thighs, felt her submission run through her body. Not wanting to prolong it any further, he began spanking her in earnest, taking her pale white bottom to a pink, then to an even darker red. Her feet kicked the ground and a wail emerged from her throat.

Her hand snaked back to try to cover her backside, but he pinned it to her waist. He wasn't through with her yet. Peppering her bottom with more spanks, he felt her body relent to him even further. He knew when her body began shaking softly that she was beginning to cry, and he softened his spanks a little, the sound having more bite than the smacks itself.

"You will always talk to me when something bothers you. You are not to hide and run from me ever again. Is that clear?"

Silence greeted him, her cries quiet.

"Morgana, I expect an answer."

He quickly peppered the tops of her thighs with sharp stingy smacks, and she cried out a reply, her voice straining under his punishing hand.

"Yes, sir. I understand."

"Now, let me help you to stand. We're going to finish your punishment with you bending over this log." He helped her up, and walked to a nearby tree. Taking out the knife he kept in the pocket of his jeans, he cut a slender thin branch.

"We're not done?"

She stood there, tears running down her face, uncertainty bathing her features. Yet in all her sniffles, she was beautiful in every sense of the word.

"No, Morgana. Now please bend over the log. You have six more spanks left, only this time, it will be with a switch."

"Please, sir, I've learned my lesson. You don't have to do this."

"Come here, Morgana. Don't make me come get you."

She sighed and shuffled over to the log, her pants and panties tangled around her ankles. Looking back at him, her face sad and forlorn, she bent over the large piece of wood. He walked back over to her, swishing the slender branch through the air. She jumped at the sound.

Standing behind her, he tapped the switch against her bottom. Swinging his arm back, he snapped it against her quivering cheeks. For a moment, she was silent, until the burn of the rising red welt began to set in. Her wail was low, and rose in pitch as he brought the switch down three more times in quick succession, each one cutting into her bottom below the previous one. In total, four red lines in parallel rose across her bottom. Her cries kept rising, and he paused for a moment. He lined up the branch at the tops of her thighs and the very bottom of her backside.

"Arch your back."

Slowly, she complied, and quickly, the switch bit into her vulnerable skin, right on the place where he knew she would feel it for days to come. Before she had time to react, he placed a second line directly underneath so that two welts began to rise on her sit spots. Her back arched as the hurt from those two strokes hit her with full force, and the wail that followed tugged at his heart. Throwing the switch on the ground, he gathered her into his arms, rubbing her back so that she began to calm. Her hands tried to cup her very well punished bottom, but he grabbed her wrist. Instead, with his other hand, he grazed over the welts on her bare skin.

A soft whimper came from her lips, and he felt himself harden at the sound.

Grasping her neck, he brought his lips down to hers, kissing her hungrily, pulling her body closer to his.

"Morgana. I only want you. Do you understand me?"

"Yes, sir," she whispered, her eyes hooded with her desire. Tentatively, she lifted her chin and pressed her mouth forward. Swooping down, he captured her again in a kiss. He grabbed her bottom and gripped her very hot and reddened skin. A soft gasp of pain, mottled with her desire and need was music to his ears. He picked her up and pressed her back to the tree trunk. Her legs snaked around his waist and another moan emerged from her throat.

Grinding his hips into hers, he nearly growled his pleasure when he felt her own roll to meet his. His cock, still covered by his dark jeans, strained to feel her tightness around him.

Her naked flesh, bare from the waist down, clearly wanted him too. His kisses traveled down her neck, and his hand snaked underneath her shirt. Her nipples strained underneath the fabric, crying for his attention.

"Kade!"

A male voice sounded in the distance, breaking the mood in its desperation. Morgana's eyes grew wide, and she looked back at him.

"Where are my pants?" she whispered, her voice a soft hiss.

Glancing around, Kade saw them in the dirt beside them. Gently, he helped her down and handed her the discarded clothing. Quickly, she pulled her panties on and her slacks up her thighs, hastily tying the drawstring at her hips.

He pulled her close to him and snaked his hand down beneath her panties, cupping her sex in his fingers. Her wetness had already soaked through the crotch of her underwear. Smiling at this discovery, he met her eyes, seeing a soft blush creep up her cheeks.

"Later, when we're alone, this pussy is mine. But for now, I want you to come for me, right now." Hearing footsteps move closer somewhere off in the forest, he pinched her clit between his two fingers. Looking deep into her eyes, he watched as her orgasm shattered through her features, her body shaking against his. He kissed her as the aftershocks caused her to quiver over and over. Shakily, when her desire finally passed out of her system, she clung to him.

As the footsteps came closer, he pulled his hand from her pants and held her against him around her waist. He knew her legs were still probably very weak from the pleasure that he had allowed her to have.

His men ran into the clearing not a moment later, and didn't blink at the sight of the two of them. Still, Kade saw a deeper blush creep up Morgana's neck at their entrance.

"To what do we owe this interruption, boys?" he said, unable to hide his annoyance.

Max stepped forward, his face one of grimness.

"Revolts have begun in Drentine, just like we had

anticipated. Our scout has returned, reporting a bomb went off within the confines of the center square, and that the gunfire has centered around the political buildings. It has only escalated since you left the city earlier today. It is not safe for you to return. I'm not sure if it's safe for us to stay here either. People will want to escape, and I don't want them accidentally stumbling into our pack. That could be very dangerous for us."

"Is it that serious, Max?" Kade questioned, his concern rising by the moment.

"Yes. I cannot, in good faith, have our alpha male go back into Drentine. It's too dangerous. We must decide to make our move."

"We cannot attack. We aren't ready."

"But we have her, Kade. We have magic with us," Max countered.

"Not yet. Lord Nero saw to that with that wretched bracelet around her wrist," Kade said thoughtfully. Morgana pushed away, only to turn back and look at him, her eyes full of fire.

"Come with me to Eridell. King Dante will keep us safe, and I can figure out how to get this metal handcuff off of me at the Hall of Magic. The king trusts me with his life, and I trust him."

Kade watched her, and then glanced over his men, seeing the skeptical looks at her words. He turned back to face her, seeing the clear and fierce determination in her eyes. She stood tall, confident, almost regal. It was a beautiful sight to see.

"You think he would keep my pack safe? All of us? Do you think he would keep our secret secure?"

"Absolutely." There was only truth in her eyes. He could see her urging him to trust her. "Please. He is a good man. He will keep your pack protected. Come with me to the kingdom of Legeari. Come with me to my home."

Silently, Kade appraised her and then his pack. There was something about this woman that awoke something deep inside him, something that made him want to protect her at all costs, even if it meant venturing into another world. He wanted to keep her safe, and would do whatever it took in order to do that. But he also had to think of his pack; he was their alpha, their leader, and most of all, their savior.

Finally, his voice broke the silence.

"As your alpha, I order all of you to prepare the pack for travel. Bring only what is necessary. Those that can shift will be ordered to do so, but as we all know, our women cannot. We have to make sure they can travel with us safely. We leave for Eridell at first light."

CHAPTER SIX

Morgana watched Kade as he took charge within the settlement. Everyone was running around, putting things in order and sorting together only what was necessary. The entire pack was working together like a well-oiled machine. Not a single person objected to Kade's rule. Everyone went straight to work and did what was necessary to prepare for such a long journey.

In only a couple of hours, everything was ready. She had been assisting for much of the day, when Kade came by and told her it was time for bed. Looking around, she had finally noticed that the sun had begun to set, and a beautiful display of colors painted the sky. Noticing that he was watching her, she looked away and began to follow him as he walked away. She ambled after him, suddenly very aware of her sore bottom and the welts that he had put there. Wetness trickled down her thighs from just the memory of what had happened between them deep in the woods.

He brought her into a cabin at the edge of the camp. She hesitantly ventured inside as he held the door open for her. The hungry look on his face made her knees buckle with need. Swallowing hard, she turned back around and heard the door click behind her. A shiver raced up her spine at the silence that followed. She felt him come up behind her and he brushed her hair over her right shoulder. His lips caressed up against her earlobe and she pressed her thighs together in order to keep herself standing tall. At this rate, she couldn't keep it up much longer. Her body practically sang for his touch.

"Take off your clothes."

She quivered at his command, but quickly complied. Bending down, she untied her shoes and took them off, along with her socks. She stood back up and put her hands on her hips. Breathlessly, she untied the drawstring at her waist, allowing the loose cloth pants to drop to the floor. Slowly, she grasped the hem of the white shirt she wore, and pulled it up and over her head, exposing her painfully hard nipples to the open air. Standing there in nothing but her panties, gooseflesh prickled across her skin and she paused, waiting to see what he would do next. He placed his fingers on her hips and she nearly jumped away, startled by the warmth of his touch.

The floor creaked as he knelt down behind her. She felt his fingers drag down the sides of her legs, until his lips were level with her hips. He kissed her side, his lips trailing across the skin of her buttocks. Her knees shook at the touch of his lips, her desire hitting her with as much force as a tsunami. His fingers locked around the lace of her panties and dragged the thin fabric down her legs. He helped her pick up her feet, one at a time, in order to take off the panties entirely. She was standing before him, entirely naked and at his mercy, yet her body couldn't stop shaking with need for him. She wanted him desperately.

Although she was bare and entirely vulnerable, she had never felt more powerful in her life. She had felt his hardness when she had been over his knee getting spanked, and when he had kissed her up against the tree trunk. He wanted her too, just as much as she wanted him. Forcibly drawing in air, she reminded herself to breathe. His fingers traced a line of fire across her skin, igniting her yearning like she had never felt before.

A soft moan escaped her lips and she whined when his fingers left her. His hand pooled at the nape of her neck, encircling her hair and then pulling softly backwards. Gradually, he increased the pressure until pain blossomed around her skull, but her body reacted with wild desire. The mixture of pleasure and pain mingled in her system and she felt her pussy moisten even further.

His hand, still firm in her hair, began to lead her forward, toward the large king bed in the center of the room. She whimpered in excitement, so much so that she could hardly notice the soft sheets or the padded quilt that he laid her down on. The only thing she could focus on was his breath, his touch, and where his lips were kissing her body next.

Lying on her back, she gazed up at him and felt a strange glimmer deep in her heart for the strong man that stood before her. Not knowing what it was, she pushed it away and focused on the ever-growing need that was still developing between her thighs.

"Kade, please. I want you."

He kissed up and down her body, wandering from her collarbone to her stomach, and even further until he reached the apex of her thighs. His eyes met hers and she watched, transfixed as his tongue flickered forward and laved against her clit. Just seeing such a wanton act made her thighs quiver even more and her pussy get even wetter.

The wet warmth from his mouth descended to feast between her legs, and she moaned, her feeling of need growing to even larger proportions. Her hands grasped the hair on his head, urging him to lick her more, and faster, in all the places where she needed him.

When he slipped his fingers between her legs and caressed her wet lips, she nearly fell apart. First he slipped one finger inside her, and then two, and before long he was moving them inside her.

Arching her back, she moaned, fire blazing throughout her entire body. Grasping his shoulders, she tried to bring him up to kiss her, but he grabbed her wrists instead with his large hands. When he pinned them to her hips, she could no longer fight off all the sensations that was continually ravaging her system.

"Hold your hands over your head. Don't you dare even think of moving them, or else your already well-spanked bottom will feel the kiss of my belt tonight."

"Yes, sir," she whispered, her voice husky with her desire.

He released her wrists and she obeyed immediately, knowing her backside couldn't take any more punishment. Visions of her lying over his hard thighs, her bottom bare to his view, turning pink as he began to spank her, danced through her head. His dominance over her was entirely sexy, and as much as she wanted to hate the fact that she had been spanked bare bottomed across his knees, she couldn't. In fact, she felt her juices flow even faster at just the thought of his manhandling.

She felt his now free hand move down to cup her bottom cheeks, squeezing the welts he had put there when he had switched her. Pain and pleasure mixed together until she couldn't figure out what she was feeling anymore.

His fingers began to move closer to the crevice of her bottom, until the tips of his fingers brushed against her tight little star. A gasp emerged from her lips, the sudden embarrassment of him touching her there overwhelming her all at once. He couldn't mean to, could he?

But he did! Before long, he was beginning to press his finger inside her, pushing it in and out, over and over. His onslaught on her clit continued, his fingers deep inside her pussy and her bottom hole.

Helpless to his assault of pleasure, she felt her orgasm take over her body as her limbs trembled with her mind-blowing desire. Moan after moan flew from her throat, the sounds reverberating throughout the room. He pressed his finger deeper inside her bottom hole, and her body climbed even higher. She felt her pussy clamp down on his fingers as he continued to move them inside her. Arching her back, she could feel her body roll into a second, more intense orgasm, and she cried out at the raw power of it.

Finally, after her passion began just to fade a little bit, she lay back on the bed, her thighs quivering with little aftershocks of pleasure that raced through her body. His fingers remained within her, both in her pussy and her bottom. The realization caused her to tighten, and in response, Kade pressed deeper inside.

She couldn't believe how much her body wanted this. When he touched her bottom hole, she hadn't wanted him to stop. In fact, when he had touched her there, she had felt free, wild, and wanton, and entirely fulfilled.

It felt a little dirty, a little wrong, but entirely right. With a sigh still heavy with desire, she pressed her bottom back, taking him a little deeper, and relishing the feeling of his invasion.

"How does this feel, Morgana? Do you like it when I touch your naughtiest hole?"

Covering her face, she mumbled her reply. Her face heated and she knew she had to be as red as an apple. Embarrassed, but helplessly turned on, she waited for his response. The silence was deafening. Finally, he spoke again.

"Remove your hands from your eyes. I did not give you permission to move them. Put your wrists back over your head where they belong. And I'll ask again. Do you like it when I claim your naughtiest hole?"

Quickly, she removed her hands from her face and put her arms back where he had told her to. Groaning, she finally found the courage to formulate a response.

"Yes, sir. I like it when you touch me there." She blushed even harder, yet she felt her pussy moisten, dewing with her desire.

"Good girl," he said, a wicked smile coming over him. With care, he slowly pulled his fingers from her. He held up his hand that had been inside her pussy, and she saw her wetness practically dripping from it. He sat next to her and held his fingers in front of her mouth.

"Now taste yourself," he commanded.

"You can't be serious."

"Completely. Now do what I told you, or suffer the consequences."

He dropped his other hand to his belt, making it exceedingly clear what was to follow if she did not obey. Meeting the stern look in his eyes, she hesitantly opened her mouth, having never done anything like it before.

Gently, he placed his fingers on her tongue and she began to suck them. The saltiness of her arousal intermingled with a sort of inherent sweetness that reminded her a bit of peaches and cream. Her body heated at the sensation of tasting herself, betraying her once again in an unexpected way. Running her tongue up and down the length of his hand, she thoroughly cleaned him of her honey. When she was finished, she pressed her lips against his palm.

"Thank you, sir, for allowing me to taste myself."

"Good girl. Now let me help you under the covers. It's time for bed as tomorrow is going to start very early."

Nodding, she agreed with him. He entered a bathroom that was off the side of the bedroom, which she hadn't noticed before, and came out within a few minutes with a white washcloth. Sitting beside her, he pushed her legs open and pressed the cloth between her thighs. Sighing at its warmth, she moaned.

Continuing, he washed her, cleaning between her folds, and even over her bottom hole. Meeting his eyes, she smiled softly. She had never felt so cared for in her life. Throwing the cloth aside, he disrobed and climbed into bed, in nothing but a pair of black form-fitting undershorts. Lying beside her, he pulled her body close to his, enveloping her in his warmth. It wasn't long before she fell asleep in his arms, just enjoying the feeling of being held by him. She slept deeply, content.

• • • • • • •

Before she knew it, sunlight was peeking in through the windows. She moved her head a little as she opened her eyes, and Kade shifted behind her.

"Morning, my beautiful redhead. Sleep well?"

Snuggling back into his embrace, she groaned at the morning light.

"Do we have to?" she whined, even though she knew the answer. He pushed her onto her back and climbed on top of her. Leaning down, he pressed his lips to hers, capturing her in a kiss so breathtaking that she felt her arms rise around his neck. Arching her breasts against his chest, she rose up to meet him. When he reluctantly pulled away, she fought a bit to prolong it. Failing, she pouted and he smiled at her eagerness.

"You know we do. It's time I returned you to your king."

"Will you stay with me the whole way?"

"Of course I will. You couldn't be rid of me that easily," he growled gently into her ear.

"Good," she responded softly, her voice expressing how shy she felt to admit it.

What was happening to her? Why was she suddenly so weak around this man? She wanted to be around him so much that she was beginning to forget why she was really here in the first place.

She needed to get back to her king. Her mission was to deliver the information she had gathered so that he could use it, not to fall for a sexy doctor from the kingdom of D'Lormere. Repeating this a few times in her head, she was able to separate her heart from her mind, and focus on what was critical to her mission. She looked away as Kade rolled off of her, cementing her decision to keep what was really important on the forefront of her thoughts.

"Come, we must get ready. Did you keep the slave outfit?"

"I can't wear that when I return to my city. I am the

king's sorceress, not his slave. If I were to do that, I would lose respect for my station."

Nodding, he pointed to the clothing she had been given the day before.

"Then wear that. It'll help you to fit in with us in case we run into anyone on the road, which is pretty likely."

Still naked, she put her clothing aside and decided she needed to feel clean first. Disappearing into the bathroom, she found a brush and detangled the rat's nest that was her version of bedhead. She also found a toothbrush and toothpaste, so she set about to brushing her teeth and freshening herself up. Looking in the mirror above the sink, she touched her chin, noticing the slight flush in her cheeks. Seeing Kade come in behind her, she quickly splashed some water on her face to cool down, feeling herself heat up at just his entrance. Swallowing deeply, she watched him as he took off his clothes and climbed into the shower.

Offering his hand to her, his look suggested his expectancy of her immediate obedience. He looked at her with such sternness that her feet moved closer to him on their own. She wanted to please him. The thought startled her and her body stopped moving. Now where had that come from?

"Morgana, come shower with me. We do not know the next time we will have the opportunity. It's a long journey."

His voice broke her out of her thoughts, and once again, her feet brought her to him. As she took his hand, he helped her into the surprisingly large walk-in shower.

"This house, who is it meant for?"

Until now, she had paid little mind to the cabin they had stayed in. Much of it reminded her of Kade's home in Drentine now that she thought about it. The bathroom, decorated with a dark forest green tile, reminded her of him. The bedroom, very rustic in its design, had furniture made out of logs, and the bedding was soft and had the feeling of satin. Everything was designed to look rustic, but in a very high scale type of way.

"The pack built it for me when I decided to become alpha. Everything is designed for two, so that when I decided to take a mate, I could pass on our bloodline with ease. It's really quite nice."

"When do they expect you to take a mate?"

"It's my decision. It has nothing to do with them." She looked up at him, noticing how oddly defensive he sounded all of a sudden. Clearly, there must be pressure coming from somewhere for him to choose a wife. Placing a hand on his arm, she decided to change the subject, since just thinking about him choosing another left her feeling suddenly sad and lonely. She smiled mischievously at him.

"You might want to turn the water on, instead of us standing here naked all day."

"Cheeky minx. I've spanked women for less than that," he said, the smile returning to his face. He twirled her around, so that her breasts were pressed up against the cold tile. Slapping a hand onto her right bottom cheek, he squeezed her flesh, igniting a sudden fire that shot straight to her very core.

With his other hand, he turned on the water and the spray rained down on them from above. The water was cool at first before it quickly heated to a comfortable temperature. Kade still held her against the wall and before long, her body had grown impossibly hot with her need for him. Still, she wanted to please him. In fact, she needed to.

Slowly, she pressed back against him, pushing her bottom back to meet his waist. Feeling his cock nestle between her cheeks, she realized just how hard he was and she smiled, knowing how much he wanted her too. She turned toward him, brushing his member with her fingertips. The soft gasp that met her ears spurred her on even further.

For a moment, she thought she was in charge, but not for long. Kade's hand snaked up her sides until they rested in her hair. His hands slowly fisted until her head bent back once the small glimmer of pain took over her senses. Using gentle force, he pushed her down to her knees and she quickly complied. Down on the shower floor, she looked up at him, his large cock jutting out in front of her, his eyes, soft yet stern, staring down at her.

A little hesitantly, she raised her fingers to grasp his hard length. Folding her fingers around it, she moved her other hand down past the base of his cock, massaging him gently. Moving a bit closer to him, she opened her mouth and kissed the tip of his member. Her tongue boldly surged forward, licking off a single drop of pre-cum that emerged at the tip of it. His hips rolled toward her with clear approval of her efforts.

She heard a slight groan and continued her exploration with even more confidence. He was enjoying this too. Opening her lips, she took the head of his cock into her mouth, tasting his saltiness and enjoying his male scent.

He kept his body incredibly still as she began to push him further down into her throat, pumping her head forward and back. She took him deeper, so deep that she began to gag a little, but she pushed through it. Curving her tongue up and down his length, she suckled his cock, feeling its vein pulsating against her tongue. She worshipped him with her mouth, her other hand steadying herself on his thigh. He seemed to grow impossibly harder in her mouth, and she felt his legs begin to tremble. She felt his hand grasp the hair at the nape of her neck before he pulled his cock out of her mouth.

Quickly, almost desperately, her fingers made their way around his cock, pumping up and down, squeezing and coaxing him into the world of pleasure. She wanted to make him feel good, just as he had made her experience many times before.

She caressed his cock before she began to stroke it with vigor, and was rewarded with another groan from his lips. Continuing to tease and torment him, she felt her own arousal seep down her thighs, her body heating to what felt like a molten state. Her hips rolled, seemingly taking on a life of their own.

She felt his body shudder, a deeper, more guttural groan escaped him, and his shaft throbbed steadily in her fingers. His seed spurted out of his cock, bathing her tits and fingers with the clear evidence of his pleasure. Gently, she milked his cock of every last drop before holding her hands out under the spray of the shower. Surprisingly, the water was still hot.

Kade offered her his hands and helped her to stand. She felt the warmth of the shower wash away his cum from her breasts. Reaching to the side, he grabbed the soap and began to lather the suds across her body. Her nipples hardened at his soothing touch. He brushed against them with the washcloth, igniting a craving with such force that she gasped at its fierceness.

She squeezed her legs together in an effort to hide her obvious desire. Kade noticed, and he swiftly guided her legs apart. His hands delved in between her legs, exploring her very wet folds. No matter what she did, it seemed he would always find the evidence of her desire.

His fingers found her throbbing bud, and she shivered in excitement. Looking back at him, she saw that his eyes glinted with something that looked like pride. Elated, she threw her head back, moaning softly as he began to circle her clit. Her hips bucked to meet his, yearning for more. Her muscles clenched as she began to ride his fingers, her sighs of pleasure growing increasingly desperate.

His thumb took command of her hardened nub, while two of his fingers explored further. Suddenly, those two digits speared up deep into her core, and her pussy muscles began to spasm around him.

"You may come now, Morgana," he whispered huskily in her ear.

And she did, with wicked force. Her world turned into a fireball of pleasure, wave after wave burning across her skin. She nearly shouted with the strength of her orgasm, her passion echoing off the walls of the shower. His fingers didn't stop moving, wrenching every last moment of ecstasy from her body. She shook with euphoria, and her limbs quivered as she finally opened her eyes to gaze up into his eyes.

They burned with his own desire, seemingly boring into her very soul. Her arms had found their way around his shoulders, and he held her around the waist with his own, supporting her weak legs. The corners of his eyes crinkled and a lopsided grin took over his face.

"That's my good girl."

Shyly, Morgana inched forward, pressing her body into his. He leaned into her, wrapping his arms around her waist, pulling her even closer to his chest.

"You know, I think your pack is going to send a search party to come looking for us, we've taken so long to get up and moving this morning," she said with a giggle.

Kade smiled and swiftly smacked her right bottom cheek. She yelped at the sudden shocking sting, her backside feeling hot from the touch of his hand.

"Kade!"

"That's 'sir' to you, my sassy redhead."

Morgana did her best to rinse herself off, and then nearly sprinted out of the shower, grabbing a towel hanging near her.

"Whatever, boss," she responded cheekily, a grin plastered all over her face. She watched as a dangerous look came over his as he tried to look serious, but soon, his mouth twisted up in a smile.

He moved swiftly after her, pulling a towel around his waist in the process. Backing up to the bed, she realized she had nowhere to run. He put his hands down on either side of her before grabbing her hips, twisting her around, and planting her face down on the bed.

"I see we're going to have to start the day with a reddened bottom for you, is that the case, Morgana?" he asked, unable to hide the amusement in his voice. He whipped the towel away from her body, leaving her damp, trembling, and naked to his view. Her bottom quivered in anticipation, tingling where she knew his palm was about to smack. She felt entirely vulnerable, yet safe in his hands.

His touch trailed up her thighs, his fingernails digging into her flesh. Arching her bottom up for more, she sighed with delight. When his hand left her bottom, she tensed slightly before it came raining down on her bare backside. Spank after spank fell, warming her flesh, making it feel hot and swollen. Her pussy clenched at the pain, and her hips rocked back and forth. The spanking wasn't particularly hard, but each one rocketed a shot of fire into her aching sex. He spanked all over her bottom, before he laid a few harder ones at the tops of her thighs that made her cry out from the shock of it. All at once, he stopped before placing a hand on the small of her back.

She heard a drawer open, and he began to rummage around inside it. Nervous butterflies flew about in her stomach. What was he up to now?

He parted her cheeks and ran his finger over her bottom hole. Shuddering at the naughtiness of that single act, Morgana gasped in surprise. Something cold spurted onto her tight little star, and he circled it around the rim of it.

"What are you doing," she cried out apprehensively.

"I have a gift for you, something to remind you all day that you are mine, and mine alone."

A cold object pressed against her bottom hole and her entire body tensed.

"Relax, Morgana. If you behave and take this in your bottom like a good girl, then I won't paddle your backside with your hairbrush. Still, even if I have to, you're going to take this plug inside your naughty hole whether you like it or not. But, I have the strangest feeling that you will. Am I right, little one?"

Struggling, she finally got her body to relax, and felt the plug begin to invade her backside. At first it hurt a little, stretching her bottom further than she had ever experienced before. A slight whimper emerged from her throat as the plug widened her even more, before it suddenly popped into place.

Her bottom felt fuller than ever before. It was certainly larger than the small plug he had put inside her before, when he had wanted to keep the suppositories in place deep in her bottom. She felt embarrassed, yet her body felt impossibly hot and her sex throbbed at his treatment. His fingers glided against her folds, and he held them in front of her face, glistening in the morning light with her honey.

"See? You do like it. Which is good, because I need to begin your training so that you will take my cock here too."

"Training?"

"Yes. I'm going to train your naughty hole to open so that I can fuck you there."

He pressed the base of the plug down deeper into her bottom, as she inhaled at the thought. He would put his cock in her backside? The thought scared her a bit, yet her body warmed at the same time. He was so massive, it couldn't possibly fit back there, in her tight rosette. She felt so wanton to enjoy something so naughty, something that no one had ever talked about. She had never known she could derive such pleasure from someone touching her forbidden hole.

He presented his fingers closer to her lips, and she dutifully cleaned her arousal from them. Meeting his eyes, she saw him looking down huskily at her. He removed his hand from her back and allowed her to rise. She glanced down at his towel and saw the very clear bulge of his hardness there. Swallowing deeply, her breathing shallow, she shifted from one foot to the other.

"You'd put your cock inside my bottom?" she asked, her legs quivering with unspoken desire.

"Yes. I'm going to fuck that naughty little hole of yours until you beg me to let you come."

Her eyes widened in shock, yet her body thrilled with anticipation. With her bottom full of his plug, her cheeks clenched, driving it deep inside her, she nodded, whispering a simple "yes, sir."

He grinned as she turned away and picked up her discarded clothing. Finding a pair of fresh panties, a pretty pale pink color surrounded by lace, she threaded them up her legs. The fabric of her panties seemed to press the plug securely inside her. Next, she pulled on the white cloth shirt and the cream-colored drawstring pants. Finding her socks and shoes, she pulled them on as well. Before long, she was entirely dressed, yet the feeling in her naughty hole left her achy with desire.

Her nipples peaked and she felt wetness soak the seat of her panties. She watched as Kade took off his towel, his cock jutting out into the air. She wanted to jump on top of him and ride it, her pussy and bottom full at the same time.

Her mouth opened wide, and her hand shot up to cover it.

What sort of person was she to think about, and even want something like that? She felt entirely naughty, a bit dirty, but incredibly turned on. She shouldn't want this, but she did. Oh so much.

He dressed rapidly, wearing a pair of dark blue jeans and a black t-shirt.

"Come, it's time to get moving. Put together whatever you need, and meet me outside. And Morgana?"

"Yes, sir?"

"It pleases me that your naughtiest hole will be full for the day, simply because I wished it so."

Her eyes grew wide, and she felt her pussy gush at his words. Her bottom cheeks tightened, pressing the plug deeper inside her. Why did this turn her body on so much? He turned away and exited the cabin, leaving her hot and trembling.

Trying to distract herself, she packed a bag with her few belongings, and with a heavy sigh, turned to follow him out the door. The sunlight caressed her skin, blue sky overhead. She didn't see a single cloud in the sky. It was going to be a beautiful day. Looking around, she saw Kade talking with a few of the members of his pack. Smiling, she adjusted her shoulder strap across her body and followed him. It was time to return home to her king. It was time to protect her kingdom.

CHAPTER SEVEN

Morgana approached the group and looked up expectantly at the men talking to Kade. With every step she took, she was reminded of the plug deep in her bottom, of his claiming of all her secret places, of his promise to put his cock deep within her backside. Her bottom still stung from her morning spanking, hot and throbbing. Struggling, she kept her face calm, even though her pussy pulsed with need.

"Are we almost ready to start moving?" she asked, forcing her voice to remain steady.

Max looked back at her and nodded. He didn't look like he suspected a thing.

"Yes, we are waiting on just a few more, then we need to get out of here. It's no longer safe with Drentine fighting its own civil war on our doorstep. Now, you're sure King Dante will give us safe passage? He will keep us from harm?"

"You have my word, Max. He trusts me."

"Good."

Max watched a few others join the crowd, then looked over at Kade and nodded. Kade lifted his head and began to speak, his aura taking on a decidedly alpha role.

"My people of the Blood Rose pack, today we begin a

journey in order to ensure the safety of our people. I ask that you trust me, and that you put your trust in Morgana as well. I know that some of you are nervous, and a great many of you might be scared about traveling to the kingdom of Legeari and accepting the protection of King Dante, but it is what is best for our people. With Drentine in turmoil, we must remember how important it is to safeguard our bloodline, and most especially, we must keep our women safe and free from the clutches of those who would use them for the wrong reasons. This journey is going to be long, and most likely difficult at times, but we are strong, and we are even stronger together," he commanded, his voice carrying with power over the clearing.

Every pair of eyes was fixed on him, adoration and loyalty painted on each face. They really did rely on him, and she could see all of them following his every word. His pack truly accepted him as their one and only leader. It was truly amazing for her to watch.

All at once, the men quickly disrobed and shifted into their wolf forms. Nearly fifty wolves stood around her, and the women came and collected the discarded clothing. Kade beckoned her over to him, handing her his shirt.

Her gaze was captured by his muscled chest, rippling as he moved to unbutton his jeans. Swallowing her desire, she felt her sex begin to throb again, the plug in her bottom an ever present reminder of his dominance over her. Little by little, this man was worming his way into her heart, she realized with a start and there was nothing she could do to fight it. The way he mastered her body, claiming her as his, left her wanting nothing but more of him.

If she wasn't careful, she'd end up caring for him, falling for him even. Shaking her head, she looked away and then back to see his massive wolf form standing beside her. He knelt down before her and pushed his jeans toward her with his nose.

She picked them up and gazed into his deep yellow eyes. *"Climb up on my back. We are to lead the pack together,"* he said, his voice echoing in her mind. Taking a hold of his fur in her fists, she pulled herself up onto him, her legs straddling his girth. The moment she sat down, the plug pressed inside her, alighting her passion anew.

Looking around, she saw women and children mounting the backs of all the other wolves. All around, calm faces looked to Kade for guidance. After everyone was ready, he began to walk off into the woods and the pack followed dutifully, ever loyal.

They walked for hours, deep into the forest in a northern direction toward Legeari and its capital, Eridell. There was little talk amongst the pack. Morgana looked over the beautiful scenery, taking in the massively tall trees, their trunks gargantuan. This forest was old. It must have been here for centuries. With a soft smile, she remembered how Kade had pinned her up against a tree just like the ones she was seeing now.

Shaking her head to rid herself of the thought, she then stroked the hair on the back of his neck. The power beneath her was incredible. Kade as a wolf was definitely intimidating, even for her, and he had been nothing but kind to her. His muscles flexed against her thighs, and each step moved the butt plug in such a way that left her pussy soaking with her honey, no doubt drenched through her pants and seeping onto his fur. Blushing, she tried to push thoughts of him away once again.

"Kade?"

"*Yes, Morgana?*"

"How many days' ride is it going to make to reach Eridell, as well as the king's palace and the Hall of Magic?"

"*At least two weeks, if not more. The city of Drentine is deep in the kingdom of D'Lormere, just as Eridell is far to the north in the territory of Legeari. As long as we keep steady in our journey, we should make it there in good time.*"

"Do you think it will be safe? Do you think Lord Nero will notice our absence?"

"*I'm afraid he most certainly will. When he finds out that we are gone, he definitely will be displeased. Most likely, he'll send out a search party to attempt to find us, but we must be long gone when that time comes."*

"We should run then, Kade, make it as far away from the pack's camp, Drentine, and Lord Nero's reach."

Beneath her, Kade lengthened his stride, breaking into a sprint in which the other wolves quickly followed suit. Trees flew by at record speed as his paws pounded into the dirt.

The sun high in the sky overhead, the pack made their way north, away from the evils of the south.

The first few days of the journey passed by uneventfully. Each day started with the sunrise and ended with sunset, every hour bringing them closer and closer to Eridell. Each night, Kade removed the plug from her bottom and inserted it again in the morning, forever reminding her how much he owned her in every way. With each passing day, the plug was more easily put inside her bottom hole. Kade had told her once it entered her without a problem, that he would increase the size of the plug, therefore continuing her training so that one day, he would make love to her there. She was nervous for when he would finally do that, but incredibly turned on at the thought.

No matter how many times he told her what he would do, she still blushed, feeling increasingly naughty at her receptiveness toward him touching her there. He would point out her arousal every time she began to get shy about it, and command her to lick the remnants of her wetness of his fingers. Every moment she spent under his masterful guidance was another she was beginning to cherish. He would kiss her and make her feel pleasure from his hands alone, never letting her fall asleep outside of his arms or unsatisfied. She began to crave his warmth at night, and yearned for his touch all over her body even more. She even began to crave being put over his knee and spanked for her naughty behavior.

Over the course of the journey, Morgana even spent some time with Kade's sister Tina, getting to know her a little bit more.

She turned out to be a very sweet girl, leaving Morgana feeling a bit guilty over her initial assessment of her. Tina shared silly stories about Kade and herself growing up, even telling Morgana how Kade stood up for her countless times. She laughed at Tina's tales, having no trouble imagining a young Kade.

"Always the troublemaker you were, huh, Tina?" Morgana laughed.

Kade had overheard, and came to join them by the campfire, a mischievous lopsided grin painted across his face. He was shirtless and wearing a simple pair of dark jeans. She narrowed her eyes at him, suspecting he was up to something.

"Morgana isn't immune to getting into trouble either, Tina. In my world, a woman is never too old to be put across a man's knee and spanked for naughty behavior. Isn't that right, Morgana?"

She hid her face in her hands, and was relieved when Tina spoke up.

"Oh, Kade, always the burly Neanderthal, you!" Tina exclaimed, yet she was grinning too.

"I'd be a little hairier if I were a Neanderthal, don't you think? Instead I'm shaven," he paused, "well, mostly, and pretty clean, or at least I was a few days ago," he said thoughtfully, rubbing a hand down his chin and feeling the stubble that had begun to grow there. He looked rugged and exceedingly handsome to her.

Morgana did her best to stifle a giggle, but failed and his eyes turned toward her, a twinkle of amusement apparent in them. Hopefully soon, they would come upon a watering hole and take a dip in order to wash off the sweat of the journey. Squirming, she did her best to ignore the thought of him completely naked, dripping with water in the moonlight.

"Something on your mind, my naughty minx?"

Shaking her head, she chuckled even harder.

"No, it's nothing. What I wouldn't give for a nice hot bath though…"

"Oh, my goodness! Me too!" Tina agreed, a soft pout gracing her lower lip. "It seems like we've been traveling forever!"

"It's only been a few days, Tina," Kade reminded her and Tina nodded her head a bit forlornly.

"I know. I just hate being away from home though. I sure hope everything turns out alright in Legeari with the king." Tina's gaze quickly stole toward Morgana's face, and then to the ground.

"You'll like King Dante, Tina. He's a fair and just man, who makes the right decisions for his people. I am proud to say that I serve him."

Tina looked up at her, her unsure expression beginning to waver. After a long moment, she began to look more confident, believing Morgana's assurance.

"Thanks, Morgana. I'm sure it will all be fine. I'm just nervous going somewhere new. I've never been to Eridell before."

"It's a beautiful place, a great city made out of white stone, complete with a big stone wall to keep our enemies out. The king's palace is beautiful, rising up for a view of the nearby mountains and ocean. I love it there. I hope you do too."

The young blonde smiled, her face lighting up with excitement. She grabbed Morgana's hands and took them into her own.

"I can't wait for you to give me the royal tour then!"

Morgana laughed at the woman as she bounced away to get ready for bed. Kade moved in closer to her and pulled her in tight to his chest.

"How about going for that midnight swim you were thinking about, just a little bit earlier, huh?"

"How did you know that's what I was thinking about?" she gasped in disbelief, pulling away from him slightly to study his eyes.

"You're not that hard to read, Morgana. I watch your eyes, the curve of your lips, the dimples that fight to stay hidden on your cheeks. I know when you're angry, when you're happy, and most of all, I know when your body is craving my attention, just as it is now." His voice had taken on a certain commanding tone, with a hint of huskiness that made her knees knock together.

Drawing in a shaky breath, she placed her hands on her thighs to steady herself.

"Is there water near, sir?" she asked, her voice far from even.

"It's not far ahead. I can smell the clean water. This area is known for its many hot springs. Come."

Standing tall, he gave her the option to take his hand, and she did. Following his firm guidance, they made their way a bit deeper into the woods, away from the rest of the pack. It didn't take very long for Kade to find a small clearing, blocked from view by a vast amount of plant life. Pushing some of it aside, they ventured forth to find a pool of water, steam rising from the surface.

Kade looked back with a smirk, and quickly disrobed before going in the water. It rose to about chest height once he had fully climbed in.

"Take off your clothes. I want you in here with me, naked."

"But what if someone sees?"

"No one is going to find us. Now don't make me get out of the water to come get you, or else that bottom of yours is going to feel the wrath of my palm."

"I don't want a spanking," she whined, pouting as her body betrayed her, growing hot at the mere mention of a threat from him.

"Then get naked. Simple solution," he responded with a sly grin.

Morgana sighed and peeled off layer after layer, her nipples tightening once they met the chilly night air. Freeing her feet of her socks and shoes, she unlaced her pants and allowed them to fall and pool down at her ankles. When she was finally naked, she shyly covered her breasts and what lay between her thighs with her arms and hands. She hadn't always been the thinnest girl, her body curvy in all the right places. Standing here, on display before him, made her feel a bit insecure. His face hardened.

"Don't you dare cover yourself."

She forced her hands down to her sides, obeying him quickly as to not anger him. His face softened a bit, and he beckoned her to join him. Dipping her toes in the water, she sighed at its warmth. She lowered herself into the water, moaning at the wonderful feeling as the heat enveloped her in its caress.

Once she was submerged in the water, she arched back, wetting her hair in the process. Kade grasped her about the waist and pulled her in close to him. His hands moved down to cup her bottom, a hand claiming each cheek. This treatment reminded her of the butt plug that was buried deep within, of him training her so that one day she could take his cock there in her naughtiest place. Her pussy clamped down at the thought, and her clit began to throb.

He pressed her up against a large boulder on the side of the small lagoon, his lips plunging down to meet her own.

Moaning, she kissed him back, wrapping her arms around his neck, pressing her body against his. His tongue entered her mouth, plundering and twisting with hers. She kissed him back just as passionately, her body giving in to temptation. Her insecurities forgotten with the wind, her body heated with yearning. She was hot and needy, wanting to feel him everywhere, even where she shouldn't want to. Gently, he grasped her hips and lifted her legs so that they wound around his waist. With this simple motion, she felt his hardness glide against her folds and she very nearly came undone at the erotic image that raced through her vision.

He slowly pumped his hips back and forth, grinding his heated member against her sex, dragging out her anticipation.

"Do you want my cock in your pussy, Morgana? Even though your bottom is already full with the plug I put there this morning?"

"Oh, god," she whispered, her hips rolling in sync with his movements. There was nothing she wanted more at that moment. "Please, Kade, please fuck me!" she begged, tightening her legs around him.

"Naughty girl. I'm going to have to punish you for that tongue of yours."

A moment later, she felt the head of his shaft pressing against her, and she did her best to help him enter her. He paused, gripping her chin so that he could look into her eyes. As their eyes met, he began to enter her, his girth stretching her like never before, her bottom full of his plug that he commanded her to wear. In one swift motion, he speared her until he was fully seated within her tight passage. Gasping, she moaned, feeling his massive girth stretch her pussy, exacerbated by the fullness within her bottom. She had never felt so full in her life as she did at that moment.

His hips began to grind against her, pulling his cock in and out of her sex. Molten fire raced across her skin, settling deep in her core. She felt hot, needy, and impossibly wanton. Her body, once a slow simmer, suddenly felt like it was boiling.

Her fingers grasped his shoulders as she rode him with wild abandon, her clit grinding against him driving her absolutely crazy with want. Hot water splashed about them at their nighttime tryst. His fingers found her nipples and pinched them hard, and she moaned at the top of her lungs. Finally, her body on overdrive, her muscles clamped down, tightening as she found her release.

He groaned with his own pleasure in her ear, pumping into her relentlessly as she rode out her orgasm on his cock. She felt his hot seed pulse deep along the walls of her pussy, and she came again at the incredible feeling of it. Her wetness and his cum dripped out of her folds, but the water quickly washed it away.

Quivering with the shock of her intense pleasure, she held onto him with her arms, her thighs trembling about his waist. Her entire body felt like jelly.

Slowly, he helped her disentangle her limbs from his body. Her feet found the bottom of the pool and she sank down until she was covered by the hot water. She watched as the steam rose into the night, the stars glinting in the dark sky.

Her heartbeat pounded in her head, gradually calming so that the silence of the forest took over her whole sense of being. Kade pulled her against him, her back to his chest. Looking up at the night sky overhead, she gazed at one of the three bright moons that lit up the forest around them.

Suddenly, a dark shape flew overhead, much more massive than any normal bird she had ever seen before. The animal's wingspan was vast, mammoth in size. The wings flapped up and down, carrying its colossal girth. Morgana squinted, trying to figure out what it was, but found it difficult against the dark of the sky.

"What was that?"

"I can hardly believe it. Something that I was sure had gone extinct long ago. One hasn't been seen in over a hundred years."

"Is it dangerous?"

"Extremely. That, my dear, was a dragon."

"You can't be serious. That's a myth!"

"Not here on Terranovum. According to our records, they used to inhabit the nearby mountains, including the ones we must pass by on our journey. We always thought that they had died out years ago, but maybe they just became better at hiding from us. Clearly, they are far more intelligent than we ever gave them credit for."

"We should return to your people, make sure they remain safe."

"I agree. Come on, let's get dry so that we can get dressed."

The two of them climbed out of the water, shivering in

the chilly night air. Kade had her bend over so that he could remove the plug seated between her cheeks. The moment he did, Morgana felt oddly empty, especially after being so full of both the plug and his cock not long before.

A few minutes later, their bodies dry, they dressed quickly, yet silently, a sort of nervous fear clear in both their faces. Kade offered her his hand, she took it, and they escaped into the darkness of the night, making their way back to Kade's pack.

A sound deep in the forest, something like a child's cry, cut through the quiet. Morgana stopped, turning away in the direction of the sound.

"Morgana, no. It's dangerous. We don't know who is out here."

She tore her hand from his grasp, shaking her head. Holding her wrist to her chest, she backed away from him.

"I can't. Someone could be hurt out there. I have to make sure whoever it is isn't wounded, or worse."

The innocent cry sounded again, cutting through to her soul, calling out to her. Something about it awoke something deep within her, something that felt strangely like the magic Lord Nero had locked away long ago. It almost felt like she was meant to go to the person's aid.

"Trust me, Kade. I need to do this."

Crashing through the woods, she took off in the direction of the sound. She heard Kade come after her, but that didn't stop her from continuing on her mission. He simply followed at a safe distance behind her. She kept her head looking straight, straining her eyes to find whomever was hurt.

Stopping for a moment, Morgana simply listened and heard a soft whimper close by. Walking slowly forward, she found a big tree, it branches fanning out so that they touched the ground. The shape of it looked like a little hut. Recognizing its form, she realized she had camped out in many a tree like it on her journeys with the king. Crouching forward, she brushed some of the branches aside and entered the little natural shelter.

She never could have been prepared for what awaited her.

Against the tree trunk laid a quivering little bundle. Moving closer, she realized what it was. It was a baby dragon. The small form lifted its head, opening its bright yellow eyes to meet hers. Crying softly out to her, the animal rose up to full height.

She realized it must still be very young, because it only rose to about the height of her shins, its wingspan no larger than a foot across. It waddled closer to her as it called for her.

Falling gently to her knees, she reacted solely on instinct, locking her fear far away in her mind. Placing her hands out palm up, she allowed the creature to approach her. She heard movement behind her, and knew Kade must be there. She prayed he would remain quiet.

"Don't, Morgana. It's dangerous," he warned, his voice heavy with authority, but she didn't care.

The little creature had reached her, and nuzzled up against her hand. Now close enough to study, the moonlight breaking through slightly, Morgana realized the little dragon was a beautiful dark red color, with spikes running down its back and along its tail. She ran her hand down its neck, feeling the hard scales layered upon each other.

The small little creature climbed up her arm and onto her shoulder, snuggling against her neck.

"What's your name, tiny one?" she whispered into the dark. It didn't respond, which didn't surprise her. Offering her hand, she glided it across its chest, and the baby dragon keened against her, the trilling sound coming from it one of happiness and contentment. She smiled as she felt her magic surge within her, despite the bracelet on her wrist. Although unable to release her power completely, she was happy to know that it was still there, hidden inside her body. Thoughtfully, she wondered if he was key to freeing her of her prison.

Slowly, she pushed the branches aside and ventured out to find Kade waiting, his arms crossed over his chest. He was clearly annoyed with her disobedience.

Looking over at the dragon, she saw the little beast watching Kade warily. It clung onto her even more tightly than before.

"I don't know if you can understand me," she whispered to it, "but it's alright. He won't hurt us. He will protect me and you, no matter what it takes."

She smiled when the tiny creature growled softly at Kade, knowing it was a half-hearted gesture to show its toughness.

"Morgana, I don't know about this. This could be dangerous."

"This just feels right, Kade. Something about this little guy has awoken something in me, and it reminds me of what my magic used to feel like. Can you understand? Can you trust me?"

"Morgana, if this ends up getting you hurt, I'm going to spank you so hard that you won't sit for a month," he growled, his warning blatantly clear.

The little dragon growled again, this time with a lot more menace than before. Giggling, she pointed to her tiny protector.

"Not if he can help it!" she laughed, smiling at Kade's sudden startled look. He hadn't expected her to gain a protector, especially one that might prevent him from reddening her backside. "Will you lead the way back to camp?" she asked.

Kade nodded and turned away, still looking perturbed at the monster of myth that lay curled up on her shoulder. The dragon growled softly at him before they made their way through the forest. Before long, they came upon the fading campfires of the pack. All had wandered off to bed, as it was late and the next day's travel would start very early.

Kade walked to a nearby tent and opened the front flap.

"Come on. We need to get some sleep. The sunrise

won't wait." He looked at her and then the dragon, his eyes narrowing slightly. "Make sure your tiny refugee doesn't kill us all as we rest."

The little beast growled again, with a sort of smugness that made Morgana smile. She hid her face, so that Kade wouldn't see the amused expression that surely painted her features. If he saw it, he didn't comment. Instead, he climbed into the small white shelter, just large enough to move around in. It was only a little larger than many of the others, and that was simply a result of him being the alpha.

She followed suit and laid down next to him, his warmth enveloping her backside. The dragon curled up in front of her, keeping her belly warm with its body heat. She ran a finger along its back, and felt the tiny creature purr in response.

Tomorrow, she would have to find out more about the world of dragons, and why this one in particular had such a strong connection to her, and she to it. Gradually, she drifted off to sleep, wondering what the next day would bring.

CHAPTER EIGHT

Morgana awoke the next day to see bright yellow eyes watching her. When she smiled down at, as it would seem, her newly adopted pet, it warbled with delight at seeing her awake. She reached forward and scratched behind its ear.

"Do you understand what I say?"

A soft trilling sound met her ears. She sat up and looked down at the baby dragon.

"Are you a boy dragon?" The same trilling sound met her ears, and the beast nuzzled against her touch. She smiled.

"Come on, let's go get ready for the day. You and I have a long journey ahead of us." A soft squeak emerged from him in response as he climbed up her arm to take his spot on her shoulder again. She had to admit, he really was rather cute.

Emerging out of the tent, she squinted her eyes at the bright sun. The entire pack was waiting outside, and a hush broke over them at catching sight of her. It seemed as if news had traveled fast about the small beast. She looked over the crowd, and felt a quiet rumble build deep in the dragon's chest. He was nervous, and quite obviously threatened at the sight.

Kade came up beside her and gathered her hand in his. He met her eyes and smiled softly.

"You asked me to trust you in this, so that is exactly what I'm going to do. Now it's time for you to trust me," he said, his voice low enough only for her to hear. He cleared his throat and looked back at his pack.

"My people. You see before you something that many of you never knew existed, and if you did, you probably thought them to be extinct. This is indeed a young dragon. Morgana and I came upon it last night. She feels that there is something special about the connection she has with it, something that may help in our quest to rid her of her magic-sealing shackle that Lord Nero forced upon her. I ask that you not be afraid, and give Morgana and her dragon the space and trust she needs to figure out what she needs to do. I ask you this as your leader and your alpha."

Soft whispers murmured throughout the crowd before Max stepped forward and spoke up.

"Is it safe? Will it attack us?"

Morgana placed a hand on her dragon's chest, calming him with her touch. She looked at Kade and then back at Max before she began to speak.

"This dragon is very young. You are in no danger from him, yet I ask that you do not provoke him. He seems protective of me. I believe he has something to do with freeing myself from this metal bracelet, the one that keeps my magic from being free as it should. I ask that you trust me, as your alpha has. I would not put you in unnecessary danger."

Kade interrupted her, gripping her hand with his.

"As your alpha, I believe now is the perfect time to make an announcement. I have chosen to take Morgana as my one true mate. Her word carries as much weight as mine. Her blood is my blood."

She gasped along with the crowd, having not expected to hear him say anything of the sort. As far as she understood, members of the Blood Rose pack mated for life.

He pulled her into him and paused, looking at the dragon on her shoulder. The beast had risen up to full height at the sudden change in Kade's demeanor.

"I'm going to kiss her now, little dragon. You're going to have to be okay with that."

The dragon snorted and looked away, and Morgana couldn't even giggle as Kade's lips descended down to meet hers. A cheer rang out through the pack, along with several whoops of excitement. Kade kissed her deeply before pulling away and lifting her hand into the air.

"Everyone, welcome your new alpha female, my chosen mate, Morgana."

Silence befell the crowd, and she turned away from Kade to look out over the pack. Every single one of them had fallen to one knee and bowed their head. Her hand raised to cover her mouth, which had fallen open in blatant shock.

Every voice rang out, steady and clear, all coming together as one.

"We pledge fealty to Morgana, mate of Kade. We promise to honor and abide her rule, as we have promised to honor Kade, our alpha male. We welcome Morgana as our alpha female."

Silence rang out throughout the clearing. They seemed to be waiting for her. Kade nodded at her, urging her to say something.

"You may all rise. I thank you for accepting me as Kade's mate. It truly honors me. I hope to make you all proud."

The beast on her shoulder trilled with happiness as his head nuzzled her. Apparently, he approved of this development. Smiles appeared on faces throughout the crowd at the behavior of the little creature. Between the three of them, everyone looked much calmer and happier with the events of the day.

"It's time to get moving. We have to continue on our journey to Eridell," Kade commanded, ending the spectacle. The pack began to reluctantly disperse, and he pulled her aside so that they could get ready as well.

The day continued as normal, much to Morgana's surprise. Everyone ate breakfast, packed up their things, and prepared to get back on the road. She did the same, until it came time for Kade to shift into his wolf form.

"Now, my feisty dragon, Kade is an Erassan with a special power. He can shift into a wolf, and I wanted to tell you that, so you aren't scared by his change."

His yellow eyes met hers, and he made a sound like he had known that already. She could just imagine him saying "whatever," and she smiled in delight at his obvious intelligence.

"I wish I knew your name," she wondered out loud.

The dragon simply looked back at her and cocked his head. An unexpected thought popped into her mind, almost as though he had sent it himself. After studying him a moment, she realized that's exactly what he had done.

"Your name! You just told me, didn't you. It's Ragoth! You put it in my head!" she exclaimed with surprise. The small dragon raised his head and trilled happily. She rewarded him with a scratch behind the ear, after which he proceeded to nestle against her.

Kade watched the entire exchange with an amused grin. Shaking his head, he quickly disrobed and shifted into his wolf form. Morgana looked back at him, her happiness painted all over her face.

"I can't believe you claimed me as your mate, in front of everyone," she whispered to him, knowing he could hear her soft voice.

"I know what I want. And I want you."

Blushing, Morgana looked away, because deep inside, she wanted him too. She pressed her thighs together, feeling a trickle of moisture escape from between her secret folds. Kade knelt down in front of her, assisting her as she climbed up onto his back. All the while, Ragoth balanced on her shoulder, his tiny, but sharp claws biting softly into her skin. Strangely, it didn't hurt at all, but it was oddly comforting.

Before long, the entire pack was ready, and began to make their way through the woods. The sun was high overhead before they emerged at the edge of the forest, mountains rising high up ahead not far in the distance.

"Wow, those are beautiful," Morgana said, her voice low, admiration at the sight clear in her tone. The peaks were covered in brilliant white snow. The mountains were a rich red color, the cliffs and rocks painting the slopes with ruddy streaks visible from even far away.

"That's the Smoky Ridge Mountains. Fabled home of the dragons and all other forms of wild creatures." Kade looked back at Ragoth pointedly. The beast snorted back at him. Morgana tried hard to suppress her giggles, but failed. Kade looked at her, his eyes narrowing as he tried to look fierce, but that only made her laugh harder.

"Keep laughing there, mate. We'll see if you're still laughing the next time I bare your bottom and put you over my knee."

"Kade! But I haven't done anything!"

"Yet… But that doesn't mean I won't enjoy spanking those delectable globes of yours until they're a nice rosy pink."

Speechless, she felt her body warm at his threat, her pussy throbbing at just the mere mention of a spanking from his hands. As much as she wanted to hate his alpha nature, she couldn't. Her body told her what she truly felt, and she could feel her heart beginning to say the same thing.

Trying to push that thought aside, she focused again on the mountains. She still had to stay strong for her people. Above all else, she had a mission, and that was to take down Lord Nero, and not think about how hot her body felt when she thought about him spanking her naughty backside.

For the next few days, they traveled toward the mountains. Morgana felt like they never got any closer, even though they were walking in that direction for what seemed like ages. The terrain changed from heavy forest, to a lightly wooded area, to grasslands. The pack moved silently, nervous about the lack of cover. One of the men always stood watch when they stopped for the night, changing shifts throughout so that they stayed alert.

By the time they finally made it to the mountains, the pack was exhausted and beyond stressed at being in unfamiliar territory and the potential danger of being discovered. They found a cave hidden from view and settled inside for the night.

When everyone had been tucked away for the evening, she felt Kade grip her shoulder gently, and she turned back to face him. At her movement, she felt Ragoth stir and raise his head.

"Morgana. Why don't we take a walk? Get some air together," he whispered, his voice husky in her ear. She very nearly melted into him, her body missing his touch for what felt like years, instead of just days. She nodded, not wanting her voice to give away the breathless desire racing through her veins.

He helped her to stand as they quietly crept out together. Ragoth scampered behind them, mewling his displeasure at being left behind. She knelt down and allowed him to climb up her arm.

"You have to promise to keep watch then, and not interrupt us, Ragoth," she told him, keeping her voice low, yet unable to hide her amusement. She heard Kade groan quietly next to her at the creature's intrusion, but she chose to ignore it the best she could.

Taking Kade's arm with her other hand, she let him lead her into the night. They walked a little way down a trail until they came upon another, smaller cave tucked away behind a few trees.

"Did you know this was here?" Morgana asked, taken aback by the privacy of the little hideaway.

"I've had to travel these mountains once before when I was young. I was with my mother at the time, and she knew about this place. I wanted to show it to you. There's even a hot spring inside."

"What were you doing up in the mountains?"

"My mother had business in Eridell. We traveled on

horseback for much of the journey. There was a storm and we took shelter here for a few days. The trees here kept us dry, and the cave was safely hidden away from anyone that might pass by."

With that, he helped her to climb inside. Ragoth clambered off of her and sat at the entrance to the cave, his eyes keeping watch to anything that might come their way. Morgana smiled at him before Kade pulled her deeper into the cave.

He pressed her against the rock wall, the slate pressing hard into her back, reminding her that he had complete control. His lips descended onto hers with a hunger like never before.

"I've been admiring this gorgeous curvy body of yours for days now. Every swing of your hips, every smile on your lips makes me want you, need you. And now, I'm going to take you," he growled in her ear, his voice gruff with desire.

If he hadn't been holding her up, Morgana would have fallen down and melted into a puddle on the ground. She felt her knees give out at the intensity of his words. Her thighs quaked as he untied the drawstring at her waist, shoving his hand down deep into her panties.

She knew what he would find there. Her muscles clenched as his fingertips discovered the evidence of her arousal, gliding smoothly against her bare flesh.

"Yes, sir," she cried out as his fingers began to circle her already throbbing bud. His body held her firmly, supporting her weak legs, and now her hips, which had seemingly taken on a life of their own. They followed the movements of his fingers, so that she was riding him, rubbing her sensitive nub against his rough callused skin.

She whined when he pulled his hand away from her, and gasped in surprise when he sat down on a nearby rock. He pulled her down so that she was lying over his lap, and before she could blink, her pants were around her knees.

Almost desperately, her hand flew backwards to cover her bottom, the air caressing her almost naked flesh. He caught her wrist and pinned it to her back. With his other hand, he slowly pushed his fingers underneath the waistband of her panties. He dragged them down her bottom so slowly that she whimpered, knowing he was examining every inch of her naked backside.

"I don't want a spanking! I haven't been a bad girl!"

His fingers dipped in between her legs, her wetness dripping onto them. Pulling them away, he held up the evidence in front of her face. Leaning down, his lips brushed against her ear, and he began to scold her, his voice making her stomach do somersaults inside her body.

"I most certainly think you've been a naughty girl, one who gets very excited when you're over my knee. And as my mate, that requires me to spank you in order to teach you to obey me in all things. Now," he paused, the silence almost deafening, "I want you to ask me for it."

Her body shivered and she could feel herself growing wetter by the moment. His hand settled on her awaiting globes—bare, pale, and very ready to begin feeling his palm.

"If I have to wait much longer, I'm going to paddle you with your hairbrush first. I made sure to grab it before we left the cave."

"Kade! You wouldn't!"

"Try me."

Two sharp spanks bit into her cheeks, which had her jumping and howling at the sudden sting. He placed his hand back on her bottom and waited. Finally, she swallowed and built up the bravado to speak. Her body shivered in anticipation.

"Please, sir. I'm a naughty girl for getting so excited. I deserve a spanking."

He didn't wait long before his palm lifted and met her bottom cheeks with a resounding slap. He spanked each side before landing one right over her pussy, and she arched in surprise, the shock shooting straight to her little button of pleasure. He spanked there again, and she blushed at the wet noises it made against her achingly empty folds.

She moaned out loud, her bottom clenching at the feeling.

He released her arm, and she pulled it back so that she could steady herself up against him. His spanks bit into her flesh, but she had difficulty separating what was pain and pleasure. With his hand on her hip, she was pinned to his thighs, and he spanked her harder. Her bottom lifted up to meet his blows, each one now firing bolts of desire throughout every inch of her body. When his fingers finally descended between her legs, she bucked as he grazed her sensitive nether lips, sliding over them with such ease that it left her blushing.

She was drenched down there, and he knew it. She blushed as she thought about the wet spot that was probably developing on his thigh from her very obvious need. He found her throbbing bud and began to circle it, pressing down with slight pressure that made her beg for more. He gripped her hair in his fist, arching her back as he played with her pussy.

Her body grew hot, and her skin itched with her ever-growing need.

"Please," she begged, squirming over his lap, desire overwhelming all her senses. She felt wild with it. Hot. Ready. Achingly empty. She needed release.

"Please, sir. I need to come. Please," she whimpered, her voice strained as she tried to keep herself from falling over the edge.

"I want you to come all over my fingers, naughty girl. And by the end of the night, you're going to beg me to stop, because I'm going to wring every ounce of pleasure out of your body that I possibly can."

She came undone at his words, her orgasm coming over her like a flash of white hot light. Her hips rolled over and over, pressing against him as she rode out her pleasure. Her moans rang out through the cave. When her body calmed, she groaned as she relaxed over his thighs, her muscle twitching with her ebbing desire.

Kade helped her up before sitting her back down on the rock. He took her pants down from around her ankles, where they had become tangled during her spanking. Vaguely, she felt the residual soreness in her backside as she sat on the hard stone, but that thought flew out of her mind when he parted her legs.

Blushing, she knew he could see every inch of her, and that he could see her arousal dripping down her thighs. Suddenly feeling shy, she tried to close her legs, but he wouldn't let her. Lightly, her slapped her thighs, and she whined as the sting startled her. Her eyes glued to her thigh, she watched as a pink handprint quickly blossomed across her fair skin.

"Open your legs for me, Morgana."

Without complaint, she complied, not wanting another slap to her sensitive flesh. She tried to stay still as much as she could, but still squirmed under his scrutiny. At seeing her discomfort, he prolonged his inspection, pulling open her dewy lips to stare at her clit. As his eyes met hers, his mouth descended to her pussy, his tongue gently flicking her already throbbing nub. Throwing her head back, she groaned as two fingers slid into her channel, arousing against the sensitive spots deep inside her.

His mouth suckled her, bringing her once again up and over the edge into a pleasurable abyss, her body lost to his mastery. His fingers pounded into her, her pussy clenching around him as her body contracted with yet another orgasm. Her groans quickly became screams as the intensity ripped through her.

Kade picked her back up like she was a ragdoll and sat down on the rock. He helped her to straddle him, and frantically she tried to help him free his cock. Her legs on either side of him, her hips bucking at the thought of being full of him, she cried out in relief when she saw his hardness pop out of his jeans.

She felt the head of his member nudge at the entrance of her pussy, and a soft moan escaped her lips. In one single motion, he pounded forward into her and pulled her hips to meet his own. All at once, she was full of his cock, her hips began to rock against him, and everything just felt right. He kissed her as she moaned into him, her body burning for him, and only him.

As her entire being grew hotter, her hips moved faster, her moans more desperate. His own groans met her ears, and she felt more powerful than ever before, because he was enjoying the feel of her body as much as she was his.

His breath, hot in her ear, hitched softly, and yet another orgasm took over her senses, this one ripping through her like a tidal wave as she felt his seed spurt deep inside her. Her arms looped around his neck and she crushed her lips into his, moaning with primal desire at their wild act. She felt his semen drip down her thighs as she came down off her own incredible high, her core clenching and milking his girth.

Smiling tenderly, she looked up at him, very happy but with a hint of bashfulness. She knew that they could have been discovered at any moment, and knew that her moans quite possibly could have woken up everyone in the valley. But at that moment, she didn't care very much, because she was safe in his arms.

Not long after, they curled up on a blanket that Kade had brought with him.

"We didn't even make it into the hot spring," she muttered sleepily.

"Don't worry, there will be plenty of other opportunities," he responded with a quiet laugh. She curled up close to him, a small smile edging at the corners of her lips. Soon she was fast asleep in his arms.

At the mouth of the cave, Ragoth still stood watch over them, his eyes resolutely looking over the valley below.

CHAPTER NINE

The next morning, Morgana awoke with the rising sun and Kade stirred behind her. Pulling her in close to him, he kissed the top of her shoulder.

"I could lie like this forever with you," he said, his voice soft and sweet. She turned to face him, smiling through her still clinging sleepiness. Feeling a warm blush come over her face, she snuggled into his neck, not wanting to escape the comfort of his arms.

"The pack will get worried if they wake and find us gone," she murmured, unable to hide her disappointment that it was already time to actually wake up and get moving.

"You're right," he agreed, if not a bit sadly himself. With a hand on the ground, he pushed himself up to a sitting position. She took a moment to enjoy the view of his chiseled muscles, the strong ridges of his chest, and the sculpted nature of his abs, and dropped her gaze even lower toward his large hardened bulge that was only partly hidden by his pants.

A low and steady growl began emitting from the mouth of the cave, and Morgana sat up hurriedly, startled.

Ragoth nearly bristled, his spikes on his back raised high in alarm. His growl got deeper and more terrifying the longer she listened. The two of them stood and made their way toward the entrance. When they reached the small dragon, Kade pushed Morgana behind him.

She knelt down beside the beast and allowed him to climb up on her shoulder, which gave him a better vantage point of the valley.

"Do you see something, Ragoth?"

His snarl gave her the answer that she was looking for. She shifted behind Kade a bit, her eyes straining to see what he saw in the distance. As much as she tried, she couldn't see a thing.

"Kade?"

She watched his eyes narrow, knowing his sight was more perceptive than hers, due to his shifter Erassan nature.

"There's an airship flying toward us. It's pretty far off in the distance, but it's coming in fast, and it's heading directly for us."

"It's coming from the south, isn't it?"

"Yes."

"We must have been spotted in the grasslands. It can only be Lord Nero. And he is not going to be happy with us," she whispered, her voice a mixture of fear and courage. The two emotions warred within her, and before long, her determination won out. She wasn't going to be afraid; she was going to be brave. It was her duty.

"I know. Stay here with Ragoth. I have to warn the pack. Don't come out of the cave, do you understand?"

"Yes, sir. I won't leave here."

"I'll be back in five minutes. Don't go anywhere. Go back and hide in the cave, and don't come out for any reason. I'm serious. Do not test me on this, Morgana."

"Yes, sir."

Morgana watched as he took off running down the trail. In a flash, he shifted into his wolf form, his clothes ripping to shreds in the process. At any other moment, she might have laughed at the scene it made, but a sick feeling in her stomach prevented anything of the sort. A soft concerned growl echoed in her ear, and she scratched Ragoth underneath his chin.

"Don't worry, it'll be alright."

She watched as the small ship finally came into view, hurtling toward them at a terrifying speed. It must have been some sort of new technology, using the dark matter energy source to push it to speeds like never before. She had no doubt that it was probably entirely wasteful too. Morgana wasn't very well versed in any of the science behind the engineering of the ships that could travel through the air and space. But, she did realize that this ship was one that few people had the opportunity to use, and Lord Nero was the only one she could think of.

Her next thought was that Kade wasn't going to make it back in time. The ship would take about thirty seconds to get to her. Swallowing the last edges of her fear, she allowed her defiant spirit to take over her entire being. The time for fear had come and gone, and now was the time to act, no matter what Kade said.

She walked out to the edge of the cave into the bright sunlight. With determination, she would meet Lord Nero head on.

The metal spaceship pulled up close before hovering a short distance away on the trail. Now that it was closer, she realized it was larger than she originally thought. Watching as its hull lowered to the ground, she heard Ragoth's growl grow deeper and even more unsettling. This new development upset him greatly. Even he knew that evil awaited inside the vessel that loomed near.

She listened as it clicked open, and some hydraulic mechanism dropped a door to the ground. A large man began to descend a pair of stairs that appeared as the door dropped. Seeing a pair of hefty dark-colored boots emerge first, she watched as he climbed down, his strut unique enough that it could only belong to one man. She pushed her chest forward and pulled herself up taller. There was no way she would show Lord Nero even an ounce of fear.

His muscled chest came into view, the immensity of his bulk still taking her back a bit. Dark brown pants settled around his waist, held up by a thick brown belt. The gold jewelry on his ear and nose glinted in the sun, blinding her momentarily. His scowl chilled her to the bone, and a sick feeling of dread settled in the pit of her stomach, but she didn't allow any of that to show in her body language.

His black eyes stared at her, and a dangerous smirk played on the corner of his lips. She glared back at him, willing him to die with each step he took. Unfortunately, defeating him wouldn't be that simple.

He stopped in front of her, too close for her comfort. She stood her ground though, raising her chin in defiance.

"What do you want, Nero," she spat at him, deliberately demeaning him by ignoring his title of self-appointed lord. He simply smiled and allowed his black eyes to stray up and down her body.

"I came to take back what's mine, and kill the man who stole her from me."

"I was never yours, and I never will be."

"Even collared of your magic, you're still trouble. Your powers may stop my Soul Eater ability from causing you unspeakable mental pain, but I have other ways of hurting you. I will make you beg at my knees for mercy, regardless. You will bow to my hand, I have no doubt."

"Never," she growled, her eyes darkening with her ever-growing hatred of the man.

She had always known her mind was safe from his dark powers, but hadn't known why. Once a human's magic awakened, that individual was safe from his abilities, like a natural shield. She smiled, knowing that he could never touch Lana in the same way again because of her magic, and that he could never invoke the raw terror she had seen in the girl's eyes when she had saved her from his clutches.

He was a Soul Eater, but even though her mind was safe, she still shouldn't underestimate him.

He was a pure, unbridled weapon of war. The ultimate

information gatherer, and the power had very clearly gone to his head. He took what was a way to gain intel without torture and twisted it into something much worse. She knew some of the history behind the development of the Soul Eaters and it wasn't a pretty story.

The scientists who made them had exclusively chosen the men to take on the Soul Eater role. Five men were chosen from an elite group of proven army veterans, some human and some Erassan. Every man granted with the everlasting life that came with the terrible powers of a Soul Eater turned good, honorable men into evil, torture-loving psychopaths, willing to do anything to gain even more power.

According to the history books she had read, they had killed hundreds, if not thousands in their quest to gain even more control than they already had. It was a dark time in planet Terranovum's history as massive civil war ensued until a group of wizards and sorceresses finally took down the Soul Eaters in a bloody fight. She had thought the technology died with the last of them, but that was before she had learned of Nero's existence.

Someone had made him, set him loose, and allowed his evil to simmer until now. She would make sure that ended before he hurt anyone else. Narrowing her eyes, fiercely determined, she stood tall.

"You will never touch me, Nero. Not ever."

Ragoth growled deeply on her shoulder. As if noticing the dragon for the first time, Nero's black eyes shifted to him, and a confused expression passed over his face.

"I thought dragons were long dead. Not one has been spotted for centuries."

"It appears you heard wrong then."

His glance nervously dropped down to her bracelet and then to her face. His agitated look passed quickly and turned into an evil smile, as if he knew something that she didn't.

"Well, after I kill Kade for the treason he's committed, I'll make sure to kill him too."

"You're just an evil bastard, intent on gaining as much power as you possibly can."

"Why thank you, Morgana, I'll remember that when I bind you to a pole and whip your naked body for your insolence. Still your cheeky tongue, you are testing my patience to its limits. Now, tell me, is Kade hiding in the cave behind you?"

"I don't know, maybe you should check it out yourself."

He took a step closer to her and swung his arm around, slapping her across the face with such force that it nearly threw her to the ground. Ragoth roared, the sound startlingly loud coming from such a small creature. He flew up in the air and swooped down at Nero's head. The man whirled around, trying to bat the dragon out of the way.

"Call off the beast before I kill him!"

She watched as Ragoth's teeth closed around the man's shoulder, blood brimming to the surface as he broke the skin. Nero cried out and moved to smack Ragoth away, but the little beast had already drawn back, high into the air out of his reach. The man glared at the dragon, and then turned his gaze to look at Morgana.

He moved forward a step, swinging his arm around to grasp her around the neck with his thick fingers. Slowly, he picked her up off the ground, choking her as the tips of her toes struggled to return to the soil beneath her. He squeezed her throat tighter, and she struggled to breathe. She tried to kick him so that he might loosen his grip, but couldn't put any strength behind it. Her body twisted in pain, not getting the air she needed to survive.

A screech sounded nearby, one so loud and full of anger that it stunned both Nero and Morgana for a moment. The growl of rage that followed confirmed that it had come from Ragoth. Morgana heard the sound echo throughout the valley as she struggled to keep him in her sights, her vision beginning to blacken around the edges from lack of air. Her fingers gripped Nero's wrist as she tried to pry his hand from her neck.

Ragoth flew down again, this time taking another mouthful at the man's neck. Nero cried out as another bloody bite mark appeared, the red bright against his tan skin. Luckily for Morgana, his hold loosened, and she was finally able to pull in a deep breath. Her vision returned to normal as she struggled to escape his clutches.

Without warning, Nero dropped her to the ground. She landed heavily on her feet, and almost lost her footing. She watched as the man took a few steps back. The funny thing was he was no longer looking at her, but behind her, his black eyes looking up high overhead. Ragoth perched on her shoulder once again, and she heard a soft purring trill coming from him. Even he was looking behind her as well.

Cautiously, she turned around so she could see what the two of them were staring at. She lifted her head to look up at the sky, and gasped.

It was another dragon, although unlike Ragoth, this one was very clearly fully grown, and very angry. Golden eyes stared down at her, encased in the body of a beast larger than she could have ever have imagined. Violet-colored scales encased its massive frame, and each plate appeared to be made of thick steel. Wings flapped lazily, lifting the dragon high up in the air. Its wingspan was immense, so large that Morgana had to shift her eyes to see it all.

Its body was a rich amethyst color that glistened with life in the sunlight. Four long limbs stretched from its belly, sharp claws extending from each foot. Its tail stretched out far behind it, flipping back and forth like a cat, leaving Morgana feeling increasingly uneasy. Spikes ran down its spine, making the terrifying image of a monster complete. Morgana swallowed, her mouth suddenly dry with alarm.

Flapping its wings even more slowly, the dragon landed on its feet, claws raking the rock of the cave. She watched as scratches appeared in the solid stone surface, a testament to the raw power of the beast. She gulped and inadvertently took a step back in fear, but then, Ragoth flew off her shoulder. He flew toward the much larger dragon, his small body dwarfed by its massive size. She cried out in fear for him.

Ragoth landed on the mouth of the cave and nuzzled up against the beast, pressing his tiny head against the bigger one. Surprisingly, the large dragon welcomed his invasion and rewarded him by pressing her nose into his gently. It seemed as though the two dragons knew each other.

"Ragoth?" she questioned, her voice unsure, Nero long forgotten at the moment.

The little dragon met her eyes, and a soft keening sound emerged from his throat. She knew he was trying to tell her something, and it didn't take long for him to communicate with her as to what he wanted to say, his thoughts popping into her head.

"This is your mother, isn't it, Ragoth? And her name is Arydun," Morgana said out loud, her voice still unbelieving.

Massive yellow eyes found hers, and a soft growl echoed against the mountain, yet it wasn't frightening. The mother dragon moved forward, the rocks underneath creaking from the weight of her frame. She walked forward until she was only feet away from Morgana.

"It's an honor to meet you, Arydun." Her voice was no louder than a whisper.

"My son tells me you're in a bit of trouble."

"You can communicate through my mind?" she asked in disbelief.

"Yes, my son is too young right now and hasn't developed the ability quite yet, but he has moments where he can tell you details. I'm sure you've come to realize that in your time with him, like how you knew my name and who I was just now. It's a special connection that some individuals develop between themselves and their dragon. Someone like that snake behind you could never even dream of something like this."

Morgana turned back toward Nero, only to see him seething behind her, his look one of abject nervousness. She felt Arydun nudge her hand, her massive nostrils pressing against the metal of the bracelet around her wrist.

"Don't you dare even think about it, you stupid animal!" he roared out, his voice full of anger and if Morgana wasn't mistaken, a sliver of fear.

"I can free you from your prison. Do you trust me, little human?"

Morgana met those large yellow eyes and pressed her hand to the side of Arydun's head, the dragon's scales hard beneath her flesh. In an instant, she knew her answer and deep within herself, she felt her powers surge to life at the dragon's presence.

"I trust you, Arydun."

"Good. Then prepare yourself."

"Prepare myself for what?" she asked, out loud.

Arydun laughed softly and lifted her head up high, drawing in a massive breath at the same time. She opened her mouth wide, enormous teeth lining her gums that would have scared anyone in their reach. Morgana took a step back in surprise, and gasped when she began to feel heat radiating from the dragon. All at once, a ball of fire developed in the back of Arydun's mouth and shot in Morgana's direction. She couldn't have escaped the heat that encased her body, even if she tried.

Arydun had breathed fire, and Morgana was caught in it, the flames licking across her skin.

She screamed as the blaze and heat enveloped her entire body. Her last thought was that this wasn't how she wanted to die.

But she didn't perish as she thought she would. In fact, she didn't even feel the burning pain that she expected to come with the fire. Instead, a gentle warmth surrounded her, the fire burning hot just millimeters from her skin. Inside her, her magic boiled to the surface, almost as though it was caressing the fire that swaddled her body.

She lifted her hands, gazing at her fingers, before her sight was drawn to the metal bracelet around her wrist. The ancient markings in the band were beginning to glow, golden against the gray steel. She scrutinized the wretched thing further, noticing the markings growing hotter, the red beginning to bleed into the surrounding metal. Before long, the entire bracelet was a golden red color, and she heard a clicking sound. She watched as it fell away from her wrist, and rejoiced as she felt her magic surge to the surface within her body.

She was free. Completely and utterly free. Once again, she was the king's sorceress, no longer weak and vulnerable to the man who had taken her from her home. Her magic was back.

Arydun had been the key all along. Dragon's fire was what it took to end her captivity. That bracelet must have been ancient, since dragons used to be commonplace a very long time ago. Looking back, she met Nero's black eyes. He suddenly looked much more worried than he had a moment before.

She reached down and held up the now dull gray bracelet.

"Where did you get this?"

"The Hall of Magic, of course. I picked it up on my last trip to Eridell, but you remember that trip, don't you, doll," he sneered, trying to uphold a false sense of bravado.

"I can kill him for you. You are safe in my fire; he most definitely is not."

Morgana held up her arm, and Ragoth landed on it, climbing up to perch on her shoulder. She looked over at him after he nudged her chin, realizing he was trying to tell her something.

Moving her gaze back to Nero, she pondered over the situation. Sure, she could kill him now and render his body useless, but he was sure to have information that could be useful to the king. Would it be smart to allow him to live in order find out intel that may be important? Looking back down at the bracelet, she wondered if it would work on him as well.

"No, I don't think killing him just yet would be smart. I have an idea. You could certainly help me though. Why don't you see to it that he doesn't wake up for a while?"

Without warning, Arydun's tail whipped around from behind, knocking Nero's feet out from under him. Her tail wrapped around his ankle and then lifted him from the ground. With sudden force, his body whipped against the nearby rock wall, his skull hitting the hard surface with a sickening crack. He hadn't even had a chance to make a sound.

She saw his eyes flutter closed and he stilled. Moving closer, she observed his body, noting that his breathing was still even. Arydun had knocked him out cold.

Morgana kicked his stomach lightly, trying to see if he was truly out. When he didn't move an inch, she knelt down and quickly clasped the bracelet around his wrist. She allowed a trickle of her own magic to seal it, and wove a second spell to keep him sound asleep for a good long while. When she was finally done, she stood tall and looked down at the man, pressing a hand to her cheek. It still stung from his slap, and her jaw protested at any small movement.

In his sleep, he looked almost innocent, but she knew better. After King Dante learned the information that he needed from him, she had no doubt he would be executed for his crimes, let alone for what he had done to Lana, the king's woman. She had seen the naked terror in the girl's eyes, seen the pain he had put there, and it hadn't been pretty. This man was evil in the most disturbing sense. He hurt people emotionally and physically, just because he wanted to, and he enjoyed it. He didn't care about the aftermath. All he wanted was control and power, the more the better, no matter who he stepped on, hurt, or killed in the process. She knew she had to stop him.

"Arydun, can you take us to Eridell? I think the king would delight in seeing that this man was finally captured. I am sure he would like to question him. If not, he will most certainly die in our dungeons."

"Of course. Let me help you."

Morgana felt the dragon's tail snake around her waist, and before she knew it, Arydun had lifted her up into the air and onto her back. She sat down in the space between the spikes on her back and looped her arms around her big neck. Ragoth jumped down from her shoulder and nestled himself in between Morgana and his mother.

Beneath her, she felt the great dragon jump into the air, and her wings pumped behind her, pushing the air down below them. The treetops rustled at the wind that was created, and within moments, they were up high in the air. Looking down, she saw something black sprint in front of the cave. It didn't take long for her to figure out who it was.

It was a wolf. And she only knew one wolf with that kind of color. It was Kade.

She knew he would be angry with her. After all, she had left the cave after he had explicitly told her not to. And now, here she was on the back of a massive dragon flying up high in the air. Closing her eyes, she looked away.

Duty was important, but was it more important than matters of the heart? She was afraid of the answer and pushed the thought far away in her mind. With sorrow, she turned forward as Arydun began to fly north toward Eridell and the king. Morgana did her best not to look back, but couldn't help it as the moments ticked by. Knowing he would still be there, her eyes searched for him.

She saw Kade just standing there, in his human form. Her heart tore a little bit, and she choked back a sob. She kept telling herself that she was doing the right thing, over and over, but it did little to help.

Tears dripped down her cheeks.

She missed him already, missed his touch, his smile, his laugh, and most of all, the calm confident way that he had mastered her body and her heart. She blinked in shock at the realization as it came to her.

Who was she kidding?

She actually loved the man, even if he spanked her; most especially because he spanked her.

CHAPTER TEN

Kade watched the massive dragon fly off due north, no doubt toward the city of Eridell. He had warned his pack to stay put until the threat of Lord Nero was taken care of. Immediately after, he had run back to Morgana, He had checked the cave first, and grabbed a pair of pants that had been tossed aside during their activities the previous night. To his surprise when he had left the cave, he found the ship on the ground and a dragon flying off in the distance. He had seen Lord Nero's body in the dragon's clutches, and a wild mane of red hair on its back.

He knew she had seen him; he'd seen her face looking back at him.

A kick to the gut would have felt better than this, seeing her flying away without him. She had turned away, effectively abandoning himself and his pack. He couldn't even fathom what this meant for them. A deep hurt spread throughout his chest as he tried to accept what had just happened.

She had left him.

He fell to his knees in despair. As he knelt there, he heard movement behind him, and the sound of a twig snap garnered his attention, almost as though it was a misplaced and foolish footstep. Jerking up, he realized it was Tina. He rose to his full height, annoyed with her complete disregard for the orders he had given his pack.

"You're lucky that you've already been claimed by one of the men in the pack, otherwise I would spank you silly for disobeying my orders. Lucky for you, I'll just inform Tobias, and he'll get to give you the spanking you deserve."

"But Kade!"

"The only but that I want to see or hear is yours getting blistered for ignoring my directions!"

Tina backed down before looking off into the sky at the dragon flying away. She squinted, trying to see, before a look of horror came over her face.

"That's a dragon, like seriously? And Morgana is on its back? I thought that you claimed that girl as your mate."

"I most certainly did claim her as mine."

"Then maybe you should go after her, to, ya know… Let her know that."

Kade looked back at her, realizing the genius of her words. He was embarrassed to admit that he hadn't thought of it himself. No longer did he feel sad at the loss of Morgana, but determined to get her back and teach her exactly who owned her, body and soul. And to let her know that he loved her, all the while as she cried for mercy during the punishment she had most definitely earned.

"You're right. I should go."

"You're not going to tell Tobias anything, right?"

"Let's just say you should tell him before I do. It would work out better for you. Either way, you're going to get spanked for your naughtiness, Tina."

"Ughhhh! Kade! You're such a brute! You men and your alpha male shenanigans!"

"Careful, Tina," he warned his sister, but his voice no longer held the menace it once had. Instead, he cracked a smile as he eyes fell on the small ship on the ground, abandoned by its previous occupant.

"Go back to the pack, Tina. Have Max lead them

through the mountains. Eridell is only a few more days away due north. The journey is much simpler once you break free of the mountain pass."

He looked back at her to make sure that she understood his directions. Her face was serious and she nodded her head.

"And see to it that Tobias takes care of that errant behavior of yours. I'd hate to find out that you weren't honest with your future mate," he said softly, yet his voice was deadly serious. He almost laughed when her hands flew back to cover her bottom, as though it would help alleviate what she had coming.

"But he spanks so hard, Kade!"

"And I'm sure if he finds out what you did from me, it's going to be a whole lot worse for you."

"You're probably right." She pouted.

"I know I'm right."

"You're so full of yourself, Kade."

"As only big brothers should be."

"You should probably go now… I can't see the dragon anymore."

He turned away, and could see that she was right. Even with his bloodline's sensitive eyesight, he could no longer see the dragon, and more important, he could no longer see his sassy, defiant redhead. He could not wait to get his hands on her, and when he did, she was going to feel his thick leather belt across her naughty backside. There was no doubt in his mind that he would have her apologizing for leaving the cave when he explicitly told her not to, and for flying away on a dragon's back and leaving him behind.

He would teach her who her true master was in more ways than one, and she would kneel before him after he was finished. He smiled at the thought, imagining her bare, gorgeous bottom awaiting her spanking as she trembled over his knees, unable to hide both her nervousness at her punishment and the excitement that would no doubt be present between her legs.

Morgana was a naughty girl indeed, but more important, she was his naughty girl, and he would make sure that she knew that beyond a shadow of a doubt, no matter how long it took.

Making his way toward the small metal ship, he looked back to see Tina running back down the trail to the rest of the pack. He climbed up the stairs and up into the cabin, and was surprised at what he saw.

Cowering in the corner on the floor was a small woman, hunched over and crying with what looked like relief. She was holding her head, and she was muttering something along the lines of "I'm free, I'm free," over and over.

Kneeling down, he gently touched her shoulder and she jumped back, fear painted all over her face. Forest green eyes looked back at him, panic clear on her face. Long blond hair framed her cheeks, lying in waves down her back to her waist, almost to the curve of her bottom. It was then that he realized that she was naked.

Quickly, he looked around and spotted a blanket, folded and put aside on top of one of the seats in the back of the cabin. Grabbing it, he brought it back to her and wrapped her small body within its warmth.

Gently, he pulled her chin up to look at him with just a single finger.

"What's your name, little one?"

"My name is Olivia."

"Did Lord Nero keep you here? As his prisoner?"

"Yes," she whispered softly, her voice thick with emotion as tears threatened to escape her eyes.

"Are you alright? Can you walk?"

She nodded and took his hand when he offered it. He helped her to stand, as she seemed a bit unsteady on her legs. Leading her over to one of the cabin seats, he buckled her in.

"Thank you."

He turned back, seeing that her eyes were filled with appreciation.

"For what?"

"For the blanket. Any other man would just take what he wanted."

"Well, I'm not any man."

He sat in the pilot seat in the front and looked at the controls. He hit the large power button, but nothing happened.

"Olivia, you wouldn't happen to know anything about flying this monstrosity, would you?" When he looked up, he realized that she had moved to stand beside him. A soft smile had broken out across her face, and she laughed.

"No one on this planet has ever asked me if I know how to do anything other than suck a cock. You have no idea how refreshing it is to hear something that involves my mind, rather than my physique."

"Well, I won't be asking you for anything other than your intelligence, my dear. I need to fly this thing due north and catch up with my mate."

Olivia looked back at him, her eyes narrowing slightly in suspicion.

"Do you love her?"

"I do. She means everything to me."

"Then let's get this ship in the sky. Back on Earth, I was a pilot before I was stolen away, and I've seen much of what Lord Nero did with this thing that I should be able to get it to work."

Kade looked at her, seeing a fire light up in her delicate green eyes, which was lightyears away from the panic he had seen in them moments before. He smiled, glad he could make this tortured girl smile.

He watched her as she sat down in the seat next to him, turning on switches and pressing buttons. All around him, he heard the engines powering up, the hydraulics shutting the door behind him, and the entire ship began to rumble.

He felt the small ship begin to hover in the air before it shot off in the direction of the dragon and his naughty redheaded human, due north to the capital city of Legeari,

Eridell.

CHAPTER ELEVEN

Morgana sighed as the wind rushed through her hair. In the distance they had already covered, she had calmed and her tears had dried. Her sense of duty had finally won out against her heart, yet she still felt the terrible ache of loneliness deep in her soul. She would remember her time with Kade for the rest of her life.

She had no doubt that once he was free of her, he would return to his pack and keep his women safe. That was his responsibility. He had to lead his pack in the best way he knew how, and she knew that without her there, he would have a much easier time accomplishing that goal. Even so, the thought saddened her a little.

Ragoth mewled against her, his warmth calming against her belly. The wind whipped through her hair as she soared high in the sky on top of Arydun, the massive animal gliding through the air with ease.

She looked down at the giant dragon beneath her, and wondered about where she came from.

"We were under the impression that dragons went extinct. How have you survived all this time with no one knowing?"

"*Long ago, we were hunted close to extinction for our scales. They brought in a lot of money, and were used in the development for many sets of protective armor during some of the great civil wars. After that, we got smart. We learned how to hide better, and didn't emerge unless it was safe, or at night, when we could fly under the cover of a dark sky,"* Arydun answered.

"That's something that didn't make it into the history book I had read."

"No, these days, hardly any dragons connect with humans, even of the magical kind. We have found our herd is safer that way."

"I'm sorry to put you in harm's way then, Arydun. I will see to it personally that no one touches you."

"Morgana, you are special. I felt it the second I heard Ragoth crying out for one of us to save you. That cry has not been heard in centuries from any of our kind. It is only to be used in matters of great danger as a last resort. Even when the two of us had gotten separated on our last hunt, and I hadn't been able to find him for days, neither of us used it. Yet, he used it in order to save you from the clutches of this nasty man currently in my claws. Knowing that you found him and offered him your protection is enough for me. Just for that, I would offer you safeguard as well. I feel great power in you, and I know that fate has big things planned for you."

"Thank you, Arydun. I very much appreciate your protection, and for what you did for me back there. How did you know about the bracelet? How did you know I would be safe in your fire, and that it would free me from its magic prison?"

"It's something that I was told a long time ago. The armband is a tool that humans used to use when teaching young wizards and sorceresses to bond and trust a dragon. Long ago, a tradition existed where a human endowed with magical properties bonded with a dragon, and developed a relationship based on faith. Only by trusting their dragon steed could that human be truly free."

"I didn't know any of that. I wonder if anything else of the sort would be deep in the Hall of Magic, in places that even I have never explored."

"All sorts of secrets exist there. Some tame, others wild and dangerous. Be careful should you decide to explore the depths of its

halls."

"I will heed your warning, Arydun. We need to find out what else this bastard stole from its halls. I hope it works to imprison his powers, but to be safe, I'm going to keep him asleep as long as possible. When we arrive in Eridell, I will see to it that he is kept in chains."

"*I will not be far. Ragoth will stay with you, and will call for me if necessary.*"

"Thank you," Morgana said, her voice quiet.

She looked down at the treetops far down beneath, seeing small lakes and rivers intertwined in the greenery. Pulling her gaze up, she saw Eridell not far in the distance.

"It's amazing how much faster that was than walking the rest of the way," she mused, confident that the journey would have been at least another three or more days on foot. She sighed, gazing happily at the tall white walls and the beautiful alabaster stone that created the city's road system. Dante's palace rose up high in the center and she smiled, happy to have finally made it back home.

"*Flying is a wonderful thing, and I am happy that I have gotten to introduce you to it.*"

"I am grateful to experience it with you and Ragoth. This is incredible."

"*I hope we get to do it again sometime. Eridell is not far ahead, where should I go?*"

"Can you see if there is a place we can land near the palace? It would be safest so that we can get Lord Nero into the dungeon as soon as possible."

"*I will see what I can do.*"

Arydun flew high above the city before circling overhead and landing in the courtyard in front of the palace. Safe on the ground, Morgana felt the dragon's tail help her off her back and then her feet settled on the solid rock of the city road.

The crowd that gathered was immense, cries of fear, wonder, and even anger sounding all around her. Standing tall, she held her hand up and silence fell over the crowd.

She opened her mouth to start calming down the gathering of people, but before she could get a word out, a voice boomed out over the square from above.

"My my my, the king's sorceress sure knows how to make an entrance, now doesn't she, even using a once thought extinct beast to do it."

Looking up, she smiled, knowing who that voice belonged to the second she heard it. It was the king. He was looking down at her from a terrace situated above the square she had landed in. Looking happy to see her, he waved to her as he smiled.

"My king. It's a pleasure to return from my mission in the south. I've brought you a gift. Arydun, would you show the king what we've brought him?"

The giant dragon picked up Lord Nero by the ankle and held him up high overhead so that he was closer to Dante.

"Morgana, you honor me. And what a gift you have brought to me. I couldn't have asked for more," he said, a sense of pride intermingled with surprise in his voice. "Guards! See to it that our guest is clapped in irons and escorted to the dungeon as soon as possible. Maximum security. The absolute strongest we have. Make sure that two wizards are on watch at all times. See to it that this prisoner cannot escape or hurt any one of my people. Lord Nero is no longer a free man, but instead, now he is our hostage."

All around her, applause rang out as Dante's people showed approval. Clapping and shouting filled the square. Once the audience finally quieted minutes later, she began to speak.

"King Dante, this is my steed, Arydun, and her son, Ragoth. See to it that neither are harmed. Both of them have proven to be great allies to myself and the kingdom of Legeari."

She watched as Ragoth raced down his mother's back before he jumped to the ground toward her. He climbed up her leg and then her shirt before settling in his usual spot on her right shoulder.

He stretched his wings out wide and rose his head high, very clearly proud of himself. He growled loudly, almost like he was agreeing with her. It took all that she had not to laugh at his display. Instead, she focused her attention back on Dante.

"Neither Ragoth nor Arydun will hurt our people."

"They will not be harmed in any way. You have my word, the king's word."

"Thank you, my king."

Suddenly, a group of guards opened the large wooden door of the castle and made their way toward the dragon. Arydun placed Nero on the ground before her, and the group clapped metal cuffs around his wrists and ankles. They affixed his body to an X-shaped cross before picking up the contraption and bringing him around to a separate entrance to the castle. Morgana knew where they were taking him, deep into the clutches of the dungeon, to a floor so deep that no one had ever made it out alive. In her time at the castle, only one man had been sentenced to that level, his crimes so atrocious that even Dante had kept the details from her.

Turning back toward Arydun, she smiled before touching the creature's muzzle.

"Thank you for all that you have done. See to it that you make it safely out of the city. I will keep an eye out for your son as well."

"Stay safe, little sorceress."

Arydun's massive violet wings stretched out and began to beat in the air, causing her body to rise high above Morgana and Ragoth. Her lavender underbelly, thick with protective scales, was all Morgana could see as the big dragon flew off.

The square calmed and quickly went back to normal after the intrusion she and her dragons made. She grinned when she saw Wes' hulking form come out of the castle, his smile brightening up his face, even from far away. It didn't take long before his large body reached her, his gait lengthy and confident.

"Morgana, it's a pleasure to see you. I'm glad you made it back safe from that bastard's evil clutches."

"Me too, Wes. You have no idea." She laughed when a soft growl sounded from Ragoth, and she quickly shushed him. "He's fine, Ragoth. He's one of the good guys."

"I'd hug you… but I'm not sure your little friend there would like it very much."

"You're probably right," she said as Ragoth growled his agreement.

"Come, let's get you back into the castle. I'm sure you have a lot to tell the king and me about your time in D'Lormere."

"I have much to tell you both," she replied, nodding. Without delay, she followed the big Erassan into the castle, hearing the enormous wooden door pull shut behind them. She smiled as they walked through familiar halls, seeing the torches lit with fire that glittered with every color of the rainbow. Magic had lit those torches for a long time, and unless magic died, there was no chance of them snuffing out anytime soon.

Wes brought her to a conference room not far from the main hall, where Dante was already seated and waiting. There was one other person in the room, and she looked tiny in the chair compared to the rest of them. Morgana smiled when she realized who it was. Blue eyes met hers, and crinkled up with joy.

"It's so good to see you, Lana!"

"Morgana! You're back safe! Dante told me he had a surprise for me, but I never imagined you'd be it! How did you possibly get back safely?"

"She rode in on a dragon," Wes offered nonchalantly. "A much bigger version of that grumbly fiend sitting on her shoulder right now, except purple."

Ragoth huffed in Wes' direction, and Morgana couldn't help smiling at the exchange.

"You've got to be kidding me," Lana said, as if noticing the small dragon sitting on her shoulder for the first time.

"This is Ragoth. His mother's name is Arydun, and she flew me into the city not long ago."

"If I didn't see him there with you, I would have never believed it. Actually, I didn't even know dragons existed here on Terranovum," Lana wondered aloud.

"As of yesterday they didn't. They'd been thought to be extinct since the times of the great civil wars, but apparently, Morgana here found one," Wes countered smugly.

"Well, obviously she is better at finding an extinct species than you are," Lana offered, her voice one of abject innocence.

"Clearly…" Wes muttered.

"Morgana, I am sure you've had a long journey and you are exhausted, so I want to make this as fast as possible. Tell me everything you learned while in the south, anything that may be useful for our kingdom," Dante spoke up, his serious tone cutting through the rest of the group's joking nature. "Lana, would you pour Morgana a glass of water?"

Lana rose from her chair and walked to the side of the room, picking up a pitcher and pouring into a nearby glass. She placed it on the table in front of her friend. Morgana watched as the woman settled next to the king, allowing him to take her tiny hand into his much larger one. Smiling, she watched as the two exchanged a warm look, softened by their love for each other. Just seeing the way that they interacted with each other made her think of Kade. With a hard swallow, she looked away.

Without delay, Morgana began to tell him all she knew, from the extravagant city of Drentine, to the weak points in the city wall, to their use of dark matter. She started from the beginning, only skipping the details of what occurred between her and Kade. She wasn't ready to share what they had done together behind closed doors and in the privacy of the forest. Dante, Wes, and Lana listened to every word without interruption. When she finally finished her story, she was exhausted and the king ushered her upstairs to her quarters.

Lana accompanied her, helping her to relax in a warm bath. Morgana was so tired, she wasn't the best company, but the silence the two ladies shared felt natural. By the time she was fully bathed and dressed in her pajamas—a white satin pants and tank set—it took her mere seconds to be lost to sleep once her head hit the pillow.

She woke up hours later to a gentle knock at the door. Ragoth lifted his head at the sound from the pillow he had curled up on beside her.

"Come in," she said, her voice thick with sleep.

Dante opened the door and stepped inside her bedroom. His expression serious, he turned toward her as he sat down on the bed.

"Morgana, you and I have worked together for many years now. But I've never seen you falter in anything you do for me. Your sense of duty is impeccable."

"Dante? Have I done something wrong?" She pulled herself up, a deep sense of worry building up inside her. Had she disappointed him in some way?

His expression softened and he shook his head gently. Instead, he gazed into her eyes before continuing.

"Do you love him?"

"What?" she cried out, her tone peaking in alarm. She was so taken aback by his question that she thought she had misheard him at first. Instead, he calmly took her hand in his and asked her again.

"Kade. Do you love him?"

"I… I think I do."

"Has he ever hurt you?"

Morgana blushed, and for a moment, she lost her ability to speak, but Dante waited, patient for her to continue. When she was finally ready, she opened her mouth in order to begin speaking again.

"No. He hasn't hurt me. He's spanked me, sir, but I've always been safe with him otherwise. He is a good man with a strong heart. Family, loyalty, and honesty are all qualities that he finds extremely important."

"Fantastic. Well, he's waiting outside, angrier than all hell with you right now. Since you've had time to rest, I will send him in."

"What? You can't be serious!?"

"Completely. The man flew into the city on a personal ship and landed on my terrace. We didn't shoot him down simply because he didn't shoot at us. Instead, he starts shouting at me as though I slighted him, and my guards tackled him to the ground. He's been yelling for you ever since. It was only when he calmed down enough that he mentioned what his name was, and I remembered it from your story, that I finally put the pieces together. You and he are a definite item."

"Is he really that mad?"

"I'd say it was safe to assume that you're probably not on the best of terms at the moment. He's told me multiple times that your pretty bottom is going to match the exact same red shade of your hair."

She hid her face in her hands at his words, now completely embarrassed. It was hard to believe that Kade was here, waiting outside her door as the king sought her permission to send him in. She had assumed that once she had left, he would keep his pack safe and forget all about her, but that apparently was not the case.

Groaning, she pulled the covers up to protect herself. Dante stood and walked back to the entrance of her room. He looked back at her, his expression suddenly warm and soft.

"Morgana, you know I care deeply for you, and I can tell the both of you feel something for each other. I can see it written all over your face. If you deserve the spanking, don't fight it, and take it like a good girl. You will feel much better and more loved by him, and most important, you'll be forgiven because of it. That is my advice to you."

He paused for a moment before glancing in Ragoth's

direction.

"You might want to stand watch outside, little dragon. Just take it as some friendly advice."

Ragoth huffed beside her and flew to a nearby window that led out to a balcony. Looking back pointedly, he turned back and began to stand watch.

"Thank you, sir," she answered, her voice barely loud enough to be considered a whisper. His hearing sensitive enough, he nodded and excited the room without delay, the door clicking behind him.

Moments later, the door to her room burst open and Kade stood in the door frame, just gazing at her with some sort of relief. As he sauntered in the room slowly, her eyes roved up and down his shirtless chest. He had a pair of dark blue jeans on, held up by a thick brown leather belt that hung loosely around his hips. His sculpted muscles twitched as she watched him try to contain the anger and disappointment that was clear on his face. Momentarily, he closed his eyes, and when he opened them, a calm expression came over his features.

"You have no idea how much it relieves me to see that you are safe," he offered, first to break the silence.

She met his eyes and gulped back her nervousness. He moved toward the bed and sat down beside her.

"They have Lord Nero in custody," she offered, her voice quiet.

Pulling the covers closer to her chest, she listened as he took a deep breath and began to chastise her.

"Morgana, you disobeyed my direct orders. Not only did you reveal yourself to Nero and put yourself in harm's way, but you left the safety of the cave. Then you left the pack and me behind, as you flew away on a dragon all the way to Eridell, without even talking to me first. You could have been killed, either by Nero or the dragon. If you had listened to me, you would have not put yourself in danger, and I could have protected you."

"I had to do my duty, sir."

"How do you think I felt, standing on that cliff, watching as the woman I love flew away from me, without a single word as to why?"

"Love?" she whispered, her eyes growing wide with disbelief.

"Yes. The woman I love left me behind."

"But… I thought I would just get in the way; that you needed to protect your pack, and me being there just put them in danger. I thought you would be relieved that I was gone."

"I'm going to teach you exactly how wrong that thinking was. You're well overdue for a spanking, and I aim to teach you exactly how much I care for you, no matter the cost. I am the Blood Rose alpha male, and you are my mate. In my world, that means forever."

"I didn't mean to hurt you." Morgana began to feel tears prickling at the back of her eyes. She felt awful for leaving him behind and for disobeying his word.

"I know you didn't. Now come, I want you to put yourself over my knee so that we can settle things between us. I promise you that before the day is done, your bottom will be very hot and well punished, and you will be one very contrite young lady."

"And I'll be forgiven? You won't be angry with me anymore?"

"Of course. I will always forgive you. I love you."

"Kade?"

"Yes?"

"I love you too."

Morgana didn't wait any longer. She wanted to set things right. Moving the covers aside, she climbed out of bed and stood by him. Slowly, she lowered the satin pajama pants and blushed slightly when she realized that she had no panties on. Her bottom quivered in anticipation of the punishment his palm was about to mete out. Her stomach seemed to drop to her knees as she hesitantly lowered her body over his hard thighs. He adjusted her, moving her upper body a bit forward so that her bottom was impossibly high in the air. Then he draped his leg over the backs of hers, ensuring that she couldn't escape even if she tried. She was held firm to him, her bottom bare, and entirely vulnerable to what it was about to receive.

Nervously, she laid her head down on the bed, the quilt soft against her cheek. As his hand brushed against her skin, she jumped.

"Morgana?"

"Yes, sir?"

"Tell me why you are about to get punished."

Gulping back her nervousness, she began to speak, but her voice remained a little shaky.

"I disobeyed you and left the cave when you told me not to. I also put myself in danger when I exposed myself to Lord Nero, and I should have talked to you before I flew off to Eridell. I'm sorry I hurt you, sir."

By the end of her admission of guilt, a few tears managed to slip out from the corners of her eyes. The more she thought about it, the worse she felt about what she had done. She should have known that he cared for her. Instead, she had let her mission get ahead of her, and now she had to deal with the consequences of that decision.

Kade massaged her bottom, his fingers gripping and squeezing her naked flesh. Her body nervous and tense, she finally began to relax a bit at his touch. A soft moan escaped her lips. When his touch finally left her skin, she knew her spanking was about to begin.

Smack!

The sound of his palm hitting her right cheek rang throughout the room and it took almost a full second for the sting to finally hit her. By the time it did, he had already landed another on her left side. Completely forgoing any sort of warm-up whatsoever, he began to spank her hard and fast, so that she had no time to recover.

Her back arched at the sudden attack and her hips wiggled in a vain attempt at escape. His hand clamped down on her waist, cementing her to his lap. His leg held firm over hers, so that she couldn't even kick. She was truly and completely under his control, and at his mercy.

This was a true punishment spanking.

He spanked all over her bottom, starting from the tops of her cheeks to the middle of her thighs. Her backside throbbed all over, like a thousand wasps stung her at once.

"I don't ever want you to question how I feel about you again. I will spank this bottom every day to remind you if I have to, is that clear?"

"Yes, sir!" she squealed, as the pain began to overtake her senses.

He began to focus on the area where her bottom met her upper thighs, spanking hard from one side to the other. Morgana struggled against his hold, the sting quickly becoming overwhelming. She cried out loud, his spanks relentless.

"I want you to remember that this beautiful gorgeous bottom is all mine, and that we are in this together."

Kade accentuated each word with a hard spank, and she cried out as the intensity increased. She knew she would feel his handiwork for days after this was all over.

When he focused even lower on her mid to upper thighs, she finally broke down and began to cry in earnest. The spanking hurt a great deal, but she was overwhelmed with guilt for her actions. How could she have possibly thought that he would be grateful to get rid of her? That he would put the pack before her?

He was spanking her in order to show her that he loved her, and she was grateful for it. Through her tears, she welcomed each spank, knowing it was done out of love for her, and to teach her that she was important in his life. Sure, she disobeyed him, and she was sorry for it, but the real message that broke through to her, as his stinging palm bit into her flesh over and over again, was that he cared enough to teach her. He loved her.

In that moment, she felt her body relent. She submitted

to his control completely.

Arching her back, she presented her bottom to him to that he had easier access to her entire backside. His spanking slowed, so that each smack hit heavy and hard across her cheeks. As she sobbed into the bedcovers, her fingers fisted the fabric, holding on as her punishment continued.

After a few more heavy spanks, his hand stilled, holding motionless against her very hot and punished flesh.

"We will continue this with my belt, my love. Now, I want you to climb off my lap, and present yourself over the pillows that I will set up in the center of the bed."

"Yes, sir," she said her voice cracking. Her punishment still wasn't over and her backside was on fire, and probably red everywhere. She couldn't believe there was more. Kade lifted his leg from the back of hers and loosened his grip on her waist. He helped her to lift herself and kept her steady as she crawled off his lap. He stood up after she was free of him and grabbed a few pillows, piling them up on the bed in preparation for her to climb over them.

Looking back at him, she smiled a little through her tears as she situated herself over the pillows, presenting her bottom to him for further punishment.

"Thank you for teaching me, sir."

"Good girl. Now let's finish this so I can hold you in my arms. I want you to keep your hands clasped above your head on the bed. If you put your hands back, I will tie them to the headboard. This is important. I want to only punish your bottom, and not your little fingers if they get in the way."

"Yes, sir. I will keep them above my head."

"You have been very well behaved so far for your spanking, and I am taking that into consideration with regards to how many times I will whip your naughty behind with my belt. So, I have decided that you have twenty lashes with the strap coming. Five for leaving the cave. Another five for putting yourself in danger with Lord Nero. And the last ten are to teach you how important you are to me, so that you will never, ever think that I am better off without you again. I will not require you to count, as I don't believe you will be able to."

"Yes, sir," she responded contritely.

"Look at me."

She turned her head back toward him and watched as his hands fell to his belt. Almost painfully slowly, his fingers grasped the buckle and threaded the leather out of the dull metal clasp. He pulled the belt from the loops on his jeans, the sounds of the leather caressing the material loud over the beating of her heart. Once the strap was free of his pants, he folded it over once and slapped the belt against his palm.

Morgana jumped at the sharp sound, suddenly very nervous over how much this was going to hurt.

"Hands above your head and face forward. Keep still or else I will start to add extras."

"Sir?"

"Yes?"

"Will you touch me at least, put your hand on my waist?" She was desperate to feel his touch, to know that he was connected to her during what was bound to be a very painful learning experience.

"I can do that. Now, I want you to ask me for the rest of your punishment."

She felt his hand settle on her lower back, his strength holding her down. Swallowing convulsively, she forced herself to speak the words he wanted, yet her voice cracked with her nerves. Her bottom clenched in anticipation.

"Please, sir, I've been a bad girl and deserve to have my backside whipped with your belt. Please punish me until you think I have learned my lesson."

Strangely, as these words left her mouth, she felt her arousal begin to drip down her thighs, which quivered as she pressed her legs together. How was is possible that she knew she was getting punished, yet her body wanted it, craved it even? It hurt like hell, for god's sake, but there was no denying the fact that she was most certainly wet from his spanking alone. He hadn't even begun to touch her where she really wanted him to yet.

"Relax your bottom. Once you submit to me, I will punish you for being such a naughty girl."

She tried desperately to do so, and once she did, the belt cracked hard against her bottom for the very first time. A line of fire bit into her skin and she cried out. She almost allowed her hands to fly back, but then she remembered that he had ordered her to keep them above her head. Clasping her hands together, she vowed not to let them reach back at all during the rest of her spanking.

Breathing, she relaxed and the next stroke came down across her cheeks. She was able to hold still for the first ten lashes or so, but once he began laying into her sit spots and upper thighs, she had much more trouble.

Each whip with the belt felt like someone had laid a hot iron across her bottom, the bite of the leather like nothing she had ever felt before. It hurt so much that she lost count of how many spanks of the wicked leather strap she had left, sobbing into the bedspread. Her hands clenched together in tight fists as it fell, again and again.

She had no doubt she wouldn't be able to sit comfortably for days, but she deserved this. She couldn't believe what she had done.

"I'm so sorry," she cried into the quilt, repeating it over and over until she realized that he had sat down beside her. His hand massaged up and down her back.

"I forgive you," he said, his voice full of warmth and love.

Suddenly, she needed to be in his arms. Pushing herself up from the mound of pillows, she curled up on his lap, her arms hugging around him and her head lying on his shoulder. His arms wrapped around her small body as she cried out the rest of her tears against his warm chest.

"You really forgive me?"

"Of course, Morgana. You are my good girl again."

Smiling softly, she peered up into his golden eyes. He brushed an errant piece of hair out of her face, his fingers lingering on the sensitive skin of her cheek. Her tongue gently licked her lips, and the hungry look on his face nearly undid her.

He gripped her hair in a tight fist at the back of her head and his mouth overtook her own. His lips kissed her hungrily, and his tongue explored and tangled with hers. A soft moan escaped Morgana's lips as their kiss deepened even further. Her pussy began to throb with desperate need at this sudden onslaught, her juices slickening her entrance and dripping down her thighs.

She was hot and ready like never before. She needed him to fuck her, hard and fast and without mercy. She needed him to claim her completely.

He pushed her to the bed gently, pressing her back against the soft surface. Without a fight she let him, knowing he knew exactly what she needed. Hissing slightly when her bottom touched the bed, she saw him smile at her discomfort.

Breaking off the kiss, she looked up at him.

"If I weren't a very punished little girl right now, I would say you enjoyed spanking me."

"I will never tire of spanking your gorgeous globes, my sassy redhead. You can bet that you will have a very pink bottom more often than not now that you're mine."

A shiver raced up her spine at his threat, and she moved to kiss him again, the ache between her legs continuing to grow at an alarming rate.

"Please."

"Please what?"

"Please fuck me, sir!"

"Just spanked and already you're racking up points for your next one. Such a naughty girl you are, with that mouth. I have remedies for that."

"Promises, promises…"

"I hope you can say that when my cock is in your tight

little ass tonight."

"What?" she asked, wide-eyed, but strangely aroused.

"That's right. After I take your pussy with a good hard fucking, I'm going to claim your naughtiest hole."

She couldn't even respond as he bent down and his lips demanded her attention, his body hot on top of hers. Feeling his hardness throbbing against her thigh, she ground her hips into his, her sore bottom pressing into the bed. It still hurt quite a bit, but her need for pleasure intermingled with the pain so that the mixture heightened her senses to all new levels.

Her whole body felt like it was on fire, and she burned only for him; only he could give her what she so desperately craved and didn't even know she needed. Even though she had never been taken in her bottom hole by a man before, the thought made her grow even hotter, yet slightly naughty, like she shouldn't want someone to touch her there. But she did. And she wanted that person to be Kade.

Moaning, her fingers scratched against his back as she arched her own, her nipples hardening under her white satin tank top. Kade pushed the soft material over her head and she was completely naked underneath him.

She reached down and unbuttoned his jeans, smiling slyly up at him as she did it. Pushing his jeans down his waist, she freed his massive girth to her grasp. Reaching down, she took the velvet hardness into her fingers and moved her hand up and down its length.

"Such a naughty minx."

"But I'm your naughty minx," she said, a shred of hope apparent in her voice.

"Always."

He kissed her again, all while grinding his pelvis into hers. She released her hold on his cock and groaned out loud when it rubbed up against her aching bud. Panting, she couldn't hold off much longer, needing him inside her.

Thankfully, he pushed her legs apart with his knee, a look of hard determination on his face. He guided his cock to her entrance and she tried frantically to help him by hooking her legs around his waist and pulling him toward her. The head of his cock pressed at her slickened opening until he pulled back slightly. She whined at his absence, the chilly air caressing her needy pussy.

"Be still," he said, placing a sharp slap on her inner thigh. With a gasp, she looked down and saw his pink handprint emerge on her pale skin. The image made her pelvic muscles clench and more wetness trickled down her lower lips. She must be making quite the wet spot on the quilt beneath her.

"Kade, I can't take it."

"You'll take exactly what I decide to give you, naughty girl."

Forcefully, he speared his cock into her opening in one fell swoop. Gasping at the sudden invasion, she nearly purred when he started moving his hips against hers, hard and fast, his wide girth stretching her as her pussy squeezed around it. Sounds of flesh slapping against wet flesh filled the room as he pumped in and out of her and she climbed higher and higher into the world of pleasure.

She met his thrusts, arching her hips toward him in order to take him deeper. His cock rubbed against a spot deep within her that nearly snapped the tension coiled tight in her body. He did this, again and again, until she thought she would fall apart at any moment.

"Sir. Please. I need to come."

"Come all over me. Now, naughty girl!"

Nearly screaming, she felt her orgasm crash over her, fueling the flame that flickered quickly into an overwhelming bonfire. Every nerve in her body burned with desire, and her muscles tightened with the intensity. Holding onto him, she rode out her release, her hips humping against his, her nipples painfully hard. His lips descended on the hardened pebbles, sucking and nibbling as she experienced the aftershocks of such a strong orgasm.

When her head finally came down from the clouds, she held her body close to his and looked up into his eyes.

"Thank you, sir," she murmured quietly, still dazed from what she had just experienced.

"We're not done, little one."

Blushing, she knew exactly what he meant. He was still going to take her back there, in a place that made her feel exceptionally naughty, in her bottom hole. Her buttocks clenched at the thought.

"Turn over, baby, I want you on your hands and knees."

"But sir, do you have to do it?"

"Morgana, I've been thinking about putting my cock in your tight little hole for a very long time. Now do as I say, or you'll get another spanking."

"Yes, sir…" she whined in response.

He moved off of her, allowing her to begin to move into the position he had demanded so sternly. Almost painfully slowly, she pushed herself up and over until she was on her knees. Looking back, she pouted.

Smack! Smack!

Kade spanked her hard on both cheeks and she yelped before quickly putting her hands down on the bed.

"Arch your back and present your bottom hole to me for the taking, and then, I want you to beg me to claim you there."

"I can't."

Smack!

He spanked her again, this time catching both cheeks at once, directly on top of her pussy.

"You will."

He was really going to take her there, in her bottom. It felt so wrong, so utterly shameful, but incredibly arousing. She was a good girl, a respectable person in society here on Terranovum, but she was turned on about the fact that he was going to put his cock inside her naughty backside. A little reluctantly, she arched her back so that her bottom hole was on display. She knew he could see everything, from her tight little rosette to the lips of her pussy. She also knew he could see just how aroused she was, since she could feel it on her thighs. She swallowed apprehensively, her mouth feeling very dry as she began to speak.

"Please, sir. Please claim my naughty hole as yours. Show me that my bottom is yours, both inside and out," she choked out, all the while feeling her folds slicken even more at her words. Her body wanted it, but her mind had yet to accept it.

She felt a cool liquid dribble over the rim of her bottom hole, and knew he was spreading some sort of lubricant around it. He began to work his finger in and out of her bottom, first one, and then two. She moaned at the invasion, enjoying it as he prepared her for him.

Over time, Kade had increased the size of the plugs he had inserted in her bottom, and she had come to realize that she had actually missed that feeling of fullness over the past few days. Now, feeling his fingers work in and out of her, she remembered just how it had felt, and how proud he had looked knowing her bottom was full because he wished it so.

Her nipples peaked, and his other hand reached down, pinching and pulling on one as she moaned into his touch, sending shockwaves of pleasure down to her clit.

"Oh, god, sir. Please take my bottom. You're making me go insane!"

The head of his cock pressed against her tight hole and she nearly came at the image that crossed her mind. Once he pushed against her, she cried out, suddenly nervous as she thought about just how large his cock was.

The plugs he had put inside her were much smaller than what she felt now. His girth was much wider, his cock that much longer. How could she ever think she could take him in her bottom? She cried out as he began to stretch of her tight rim of muscles, clenching down as he tried to enter her.

"Please! It hurts!"

"Relax, my little redhead. Push against me, just like you do with the plugs I've put in your bottom plenty of times

SARA FIELDS

before, and you will be able to take me. Bear down, sweet one."

Hearing his voice helped her to relax, and she began to follow his direction. Before long, the head of his cock was inside her, and he pressed the rest of his length slowly into her stretching bottom. Once he was fully seated, he bent over and kissed her shoulder.

"See? I knew you were ready. Such a good girl."

He began to pump his cock in and out of her bottom hole, his hands holding firmly onto her hips. Each time his hips met her bottom cheeks, the sting of her recent punishment flared anew, heightening her desire even more. She moaned with the pleasure of it, feeling incredibly full. The plugs he had inserted inside her were not even close to his size, and especially weren't as long as his shaft, but everything was wonderful. It felt amazing. He had been right. Arching into him, she pumped her hips back to meet his, taking him deeper and deeper.

"You're so tight!" he whispered into her ear. Reaching around, his fingers began to circle around her pulsating clit, and she moaned loudly. Feelings of desire raced through her system and she nearly cried at the intensity of it all. Her pussy clenched with pleasure as he pressed down on her sensitive bud.

"Kade, please let me come," she begged, her voice tense from holding back for so long already.

"Not yet. Don't you dare come yet."

She cried out as her pleasure buzzed throughout her body, straining to be set free. Her bottom clenched as she tried to hold back, which only seemed to heighten everything tenfold. She felt so wild and wicked for enjoying something like this so much, something so incredibly naughty.

He pressed down on her clit, and then pinched it between his fingers. He began to roll his fingers around it, and she felt like she could climb the walls, her need was so great.

"Now, my naughty minx. Come with me."

The sound of his voice fueled her release as he pinched, rolled, and circled her sensitive bud, wringing out every prolonged moment of pleasure that he possibly could from her ravenous body.

She came harder than she ever had before, her bottom full of her mate's cock, almost as though a coil had snapped inside of her. She'd been spanked and taken in more ways than she could have imagined. Her bottom sore, both inside and out, she moaned against him, riding his length as her pleasure took over her entire sense of being. She came again when she felt him stiffen with the strength of his release. He pumped into her once, then twice, groaning as he hurtled over the precipice into his own world of pleasure. She cried out as she felt his hot seed shoot deep into her bottom, and her head spun with crazy desire. Her pussy clenched as she felt her wetness drip down her thighs, evidence of just how much she had enjoyed herself so clear that even she couldn't have denied it.

Her hips rocked and her thighs quivered when her body finally began to calm. The aftershocks of her orgasm continued to tremor through her, like an earthquake that just didn't want to quit. Kade took her into his arms and helped guide her to the surface of the bed. Her limbs weak from the excursion of having three incredible orgasms had taken its toll, and she didn't fight him as he took care of her. She laid back as he picked up a cloth and cleaned off her thighs and pussy of the remnants of their lovemaking.

She smiled up at him, gasping as the fabric dragged across her still sensitive flesh, causing even more aftershocks to rake through her body. Moaning, she melted into the soft quilt at her back, her limbs numb from everything that had just happened between the two of them. Her bottom pressed against the fabric, still sore, but she was hardly aware of it. Her body felt as though it had been sucked up and shot out of a massive tornado. She felt too good as he took her into his arms, his body warm against her own. She realized she was happy, and most important, she felt completely owned by her mate.

"Kade?"

"What is it, my beautiful redhead?"

"I love you."

"I love you too," Kade whispered in her ear, his breath tickling. She smiled as she curled in closer to him.

It didn't take long for the two of them to fall asleep in each other's arms as the moons rose high in the night sky.

CHAPTER TWELVE

Lord Nero lifted his head, taking in the dark abyss he had been thrown in by Dante's guards. He had been slightly aware of his surroundings when they took him down here, only remembering flight after flight of stairs until they reached their destination deep underground. Smelling the dank soil and rot of the dungeon, he opened his eyes wide as they adjusted to the dim light of the lantern nearby. He noticed that it was real fire, and not even magic. Apparently, King Dante and his guards had taken every precaution. He couldn't even use the magical fire to help heal himself.

Sneering at the handcuffs that held his wrists overhead, he tried to pull them free, but they were tight, biting into his skin at this small movement. He could bet that they were already bruised from the thick metal.

Sighing, he closed his eyes and steadied his breath, finding the power deep within him. He felt it, and massaged it awake. Before long, he felt the darkness take over him as he embraced the shadows inside. Being a Soul Eater, he could store his powers for use at any time, and he always kept an extra piece of them kept away for emergency purposes.

He smiled ominously as his body took shadow form and

slipped out of the handcuffs that had held him captive. He almost laughed at the sight of the metal bracelet around his wrist. It was a magical device specifically created to limit a wizard's or sorceress's magic, but not his. His powers were different, fueled by dangerous and dark magic, not the magic of light that gifted the humans on the planet. His powers also had been developed with the help of genetic engineering, written straight into his DNA. If he ever bred with a female, his sons would inherit the powers of a Soul Eater as well.

Smiling, he imagined Morgana's tight little body, imagined her form underneath his as he took what he wanted and she begged for more, despite her protests at first. He thought about her curvy bottom and what it would look like naked over his lap, awaiting a spanking from his very own hand. He felt his balls tighten and his dick harden. He would take her one day; he was sure of it.

Glaring at the metal bracelet, he placed two fingers to it and mumbled a few words as he shot his own magic into it. The bracelet unclasped and fell away onto the floor. He picked it up and put it in his pocket, not knowing if it could come in handy at any point in the near future. With any luck, it would be back around Morgana's wrist before morning, and she would be getting the punishment of her life once they returned to Drentine.

She would pay for her treachery. He would make sure of that. And so would that traitor of a doctor, Kade.

Walking through the cell, he approached the bars that locked him inside. On a chair outside his prison, two men sat at a table, their backs to him. One of them was snoring, the other was reading a book. Neither seemed that invested in their guard duties.

Luck was certainly on his side tonight, now wasn't it.

Ebbing into his shadow form, he walked right through the metal bars. There was not a prison in the world that could jail him. Very few people knew what made a Soul Eater weak; in fact, they were probably all dead, and he aimed to keep it that way. There was no way in the world he was going to tell anyone what it was either.

Everyone was terrified of the mysteries of his power, and that was exactly how he liked it. Walking up behind the guard, he grabbed the one who was reading and snapped his neck. The other woke up groggily at the sudden sound, but it was too late. Lord Nero killed him too.

He laughed at the weakness of the sad attempt to keep him imprisoned. He had expected more out of the great King Dante. Clearly, these people were lulled into a false sense of confidence at the security of their dungeon and who was he to fail to take advantage of that!

Smiling dangerously, he began the long climb up the stairs, killing anyone he met along the way. King Dante would certainly realize his mistake when the sun rose and he saw the aftermath of his escape. He would see exactly how many bodies piled up when he tried to mess with the great Lord Nero.

When he finally reached the surface after losing count of how many floors he climbed, he kicked open the door and walked right out into the fresh night air. The city of Eridell was quiet, everybody asleep in his or her bed. He looked behind him at the castle rising high overhead, and squinted when he saw movement on the terrace above.

His eyes wide with alarm at being discovered, he knew he had to investigate. If someone saw him and reported him now, he didn't quite have enough power stored in order to hide in the shadows until he escaped the city.

Instead, he began climbing the wall, his muscles bringing him high before he began to sense any sort of fatigue. He was a big guy and carried around a lot of strength. It didn't take long to scale the wall, and before long, he had pulled himself up and over the ledge. Silently, he knelt low and listened for any sort of sound. Moments later, he heard the soft scrape of a foot moving in the distance, not far off.

If he wasn't mistaken, it sounded like a woman's step, a tiny foot encased in a satin slipper. He heard the sound again and smiled, sure of it now.

There was a woman in his grasp, ripe for the taking. And he would certainly take care of that.

Creeping forward silently, he moved toward the sound. His dark eyes picked up the light of the moons, and he saw a feminine form leaning over the ledge not far away.

She wore a floor-length nightgown in a beautiful sheer red color that allowed her pale skin to shin through. The fabric hugged around her curves, her full breasts and delightful bottom shaped for his viewing pleasure. If she was his girl, he would beat her silly for walking around as she was, especially without him by her side.

He looked on as her blond hair cascaded down her back. He couldn't see her face, but knew she had to have a pretty look to match the beautiful body she had underneath her lingerie.

He crept closer, off to her right side in order to see if he could get a glimpse of her face. Keeping silent, he took in her smooth moonlit features, chestnut-colored eyes looking off into the distance. Her hair was wavy and framed her face beautifully. Noticing a thin leather collar around her throat, he smiled as he finally recognized her.

It was Emma.

He had held a knife to her throat and she had quivered in fear under his hand. And it had been delicious. He couldn't believe his luck. His dick hardened at the thought of his blade against her soft skin. He couldn't wait to do it again.

He moved behind her, yet she still didn't stir. Her gaze was somewhere far away, looking off into the mountains. Whatever she was thinking about, she was most definitely preoccupied.

His fist shot out, grabbing her hair and spinning her around. She yelped softly before his other hand clapped over her mouth, suppressing any other sound she would have had the chance to make.

Emma's eyes opened wide as she took in his face. He

knew she recognized his black eyes and his strong grip, a familiar touch from not long ago. Once she realized who he was, she screamed, but the sound was dulled by his hand. Her hands tried to grasp his wrist, but she couldn't escape his strength. She was trapped.

Lord Nero allowed his power to flow into her mind, exploring every turn for any and all bad memories she had locked away. Taking a deep breath, he allowed his own magic to grow with the strength of her sadness, his power growing by the second.

She screamed with pain until her eyes rolled back in her head. She had fainted. A cruel smile came across his lips as he stared down at the limp body in his arms. Hell, he wasn't going to leave Eridell without a bang, and he would make sure King Dante was fully aware of it by the time he left.

CHAPTER THIRTEEN

Dante gripped Lana's warm body closer to his own as she tossed and turned in his bed. She looked to be having some sort of nightmare, but he could not seem to wake her. Instead, he tried to comfort her with his body heat, and his arms locked around her. A soft groan met his ears, and he brushed a lock of hair out of her face.

She was sweating.

A measure of alarm passed through him as he tried to shake her awake, having little luck for a long while. Ten minutes must have passed before she shot straight up to a seated position and opened her eyes.

He was taken aback when he realized that they were completely white. Her lips opened and a voice different from her own began to speak. It seemed a sound not of this world, and it unsettled him a great deal. The only other time he had heard such a voice had been when Morgana had spoken the prophecy in which he had been foretold to kill Lana. Thankfully, the results of the prophecy had only been her gaining access to her magical powers, and not her actual death.

"This night, true evil walks the castle walls,

Innocence ensnared will be sacrificed under the light of the three moons,
Captured by shadow,
And released only by the pain of death,
Only then, will the one true king recognize,
The true danger of darkness,
And his commander will be left alone in this world,
To find his true match.
It is up to the king, the wolf, and the commander to recognize the hidden power in plain sight,
And rid the world of shadow once and for all."

Dante's eyes grew wide, recognizing the terrifying verses from a book of prophecy that had been discarded long ago. He had read it only once, and it had left him deeply unsettled. Lana's eyes flew shut and then opened, revealing her ocean blue eyes to his once again.

"Lana, are you alright?"

"Yes," she said groggily. "What just happened?"

"You spoke a very old and dangerous prophecy. And the last time any sort of prophecy was spoken by a sorceress, the events came true without delay. Something is going to happen tonight, I have no doubt."

It did not take long for the words of the fate to begin to take effect. His gaze tore to the door as it slammed open, the wooden door frame crashing into the wall behind it. Standing in the entrance, highlighted by moonlight, was a feminine form. Dante breathed a sigh of relief once he realized who it was.

"Emma, get back to bed. Wes is going to be looking for you, and when he realizes you've been walking the halls, nearly naked, you are going to be in for one hell of a punishment. I know Wes, and he doesn't like to parade around his women."

Emma didn't respond, but moved further into the room. Dante narrowed his eyes, suddenly suspicious. Something was wrong with her; her movements were foreign, her demure nature masked by something else, something darker.

His eyes met hers, and he knew instantly what was wrong. Her eyes were completely black, the color of shadowy obsidian. She was possessed by Lord Nero's powers. A sick feeling began to develop deep in his stomach. This wasn't good.

Dante jumped out of bed, and Lana was not far behind him. He could feel her power begin to crackle throughout the air, a purple aura emanating from her skin. Placing a hand behind him, he steadied her so that his body shielded hers. There was no way he would allow her to put herself in danger, especially if he was there to protect her.

"What do you want, Lord Nero?"

Emma's body released a strange malicious sort of cackle, and Dante nearly growled in disgust as the hands that controlled her body began to grope her breasts, pinching and pulling on her nipples as a bizarre sense of glee took over the woman's face.

It wasn't her though, it was Lord Nero.

"Keep your hands off her, you bastard."

"Thought you could keep me imprisoned in your sad excuse for a dungeon, huh? Maybe you should have left better guards who didn't decide it was time for a nap when they were supposed to be looking over me, huh."

Dante surged forward with a growl, but stopped once Nero held up Emma's small, childlike hand.

"You might want to hire a few new guards; I think I killed about ten or so in my escape from that jail cell you call a dungeon. But it's not really your fault that you thought you could contain me. I mean, you don't really know what I'm capable of, now do you?"

"Leave Emma out of this. The fight is between you and me, not the women."

A chilling smile graced the woman's face, unnerving as the black-as-night eyes settled on his, and his alone.

"I just wanted to remind you, my all powerful king, that

you are not the only power on our planet. Instead, you have me to worry about. I will see to it that I personally take your seat on the throne, and bed your woman in the near future. Remember that when you fall asleep at night."

A cold chill passed across the room as a black cloud emerged from Emma's throat. Her eyes cleared, once again light brown, before they tore open, wide with pain. Her mouth opened with a silent scream as her hands flew to her throat. She grasped at the invisible hand that held her airway shut, keeping air from filling her lungs.

Lana rushed forward, pressing past him to the suffering girl. He grabbed her and held her close to him, knowing that there was nothing they could do to save Emma. It was already too late. The moment Lord Nero had entered the girl's body; her fate was sealed.

Lana screamed as he forced her to look away, holding her head so that she was staring into his neck. Her small fists pounded on his chest as she began to cry, her tears streaking down her cheeks. Dante tore his eyes away from the dying woman, only looking back when he heard a thump on the floor.

Emma's body lay still and unmoving on the floor, and the strange chill left the room. The black shadow was gone, but all that it left behind was sadness and emptiness. Lord Nero was gone, most likely having gained enough power from taking over Emma's mind to escape far away, most likely all the way back to Drentine.

He held Lana close as she fought him to return to Emma's side. He yelled out for his guards and they rushed to his door, their fists thumping over their hearts in respect. Their faces dropped when they saw the still form lying on the floor.

"Get Wes, now. See to it that he has a chance to say goodbye to her before she is buried."

"Yes, my king."

One of the guards hurried off, while another lifted Emma's small body with little effort. He held her to his chest and looked up at the king, and at Lana's tear-streaked face.

"I'm sorry for your loss. She was well liked within the castle, and I will see to it that she is treated with respect, and buried in a place full of light and wild flowers."

"Thank you."

Neither Dante nor Lana slept that night. She held close to him when they heard Wes' cry of grief at the loss of his submissive human. It was a sound that he couldn't ever mask from his mind, so heart-wrenching and sad that even a strong drink couldn't alleviate it.

Dante woke up the entire guard, and soldiers were posted at every door of the castle. He needed to make sure his people remained safe. He never allowed Lana to leave his side. There was no way Nero was going to sink his claws into his woman tonight, or ever.

Morgana and Kade awoke when he summoned them and joined them in his sitting room. Everyone was numb from the events that had just occurred. Morgana began to cry, blaming herself for Emma's death, and Dante did his best to assure her that she could never have known what Nero was capable of. He hadn't even known himself. If anything, he just began to get angry.

Hours later, Wes knocked on the door, his ice blue eyes red with his loss.

"Mind if I join you for a drink?"

"Anytime, brother. Come, have a glass of whiskey with me, so that we may celebrate Emma's life, rather than focus on her loss."

"I don't know if I can, my king."

"Then, let us drink, and think of how we will find our revenge on Lord Nero and the empire of D'Lormere."

"Now that is something I can raise a glass to," Wes said, his face hardening with anger and purpose. "I vow that before I take my last breath, Lord Nero will be long dead for the evil he has done. I will avenge my Emma."

Dante, Lana, Kade, and Morgana all raised their glasses

with Wes. Every single face had a look of grim determination. Lord Nero wouldn't stand a chance with all of them banded together.

EPILOGUE

It took many days for Wes to feel like life was back to normal. He struggled from day to day, each morning expecting his sweet obedient Emma to be there at his beck and call, only to remember she had died at the hands of Lord Nero. Dante, Lana, Morgana, and Kade all gave him a wide berth as he struggled with his grief. The only thing he could focus on was their growing plan of attack on the enemy, deep within the territory of D'Lormere.

Kade's pack arrived a few days after the attack, and settled in a guarded district in a sparse settlement of the city. Wes didn't give them much thought.

The entire castle seemed quiet around him, almost as though they were walking on eggshells whenever they entered the room. Finally, when he couldn't stand it any longer, he went back to his job of processing captured human females for auction, just so that he would have something to keep himself busy and so that he could feel some semblance of control.

Every day, he had to calm another human. Some of them would cooperate with simply a stern look, and with others he had to take firmer measures, such as a spanking, either on the bare or over clothing. Sure, he enjoyed the time he spent there, but he felt hollow without his demure submissive waiting for him in his bed.

It took almost a year for him to feel somewhat normal again. In that time, little had been heard from either Lord Nero or any of his minions in D'Lormere. The uprising in Drentine had been quelled in record time after Morgana and Kade had arrived. For some while now, there had been a sort of unsteady peace on the planet and life had gotten back to normal.

But then one day, he came upon a pair of green eyes hidden deep within one of the holding cells. Blond wavy hair framed high cheekbones and delicate pink lips. Long lashes outlined soft eyes that trembled whenever a man looked upon her, and left him longing to learn more about her. She had met his eyes for but a moment and then looked away at the floor, nearly shaking with fear at being spotted.

He had made his decision then and there. He pointed to her and decided that she would be next in the line for humans prepared for auction. The moment she realized she had been picked out of the crowd, she had fought like a wild animal, legs kicking and fists slamming into anyone who wandered near.

Multiple large Erassans had needed to come forth to hold her panicked limbs. Wild eyes stared back at him as he walked up to her. Something about the way she looked back at him called out to his heart, awakening a savage need inside him to protect this small tiny human female. He swallowed back the need to bare her completely and spank her rebellious bottom until it was bright red and swollen to the touch.

"What is your name, my ferocious human girl?"

"My name is Olivia. And I am most certainly not your girl," she growled in response. He smiled at her minor attempt at sassing him, and he grew more interested by the second.

"Well, Olivia, we're going to have to see about that, now won't we. See to it that she is bathed and prepared for examination. We must assess whether she is a healthy female, both inside and out. And then, we will prepare her for auction. I am to be informed about her progress every step of the way. I have a feeling that Olivia and I will know each other rather intimately before she is brought up for sale."

Her beautiful green eyes glared back at him, both intrigued and rebellious at the same time. She looked like she was about to growl at him.

"Who are you," she whispered, trepidation clear in her tone.

"My name is Wes. And I will oversee your training as a slave in King Dante's palace. Pleased to meet you," he said, a wicked smile of anticipation overtaking his lips. He couldn't wait to see what this wild human had hidden beneath the grimy clothes that covered her slender frame.

For the first time in many, many months, he looked forward to what the next day might bring.

THE END

MAP OF TERRANOVUM

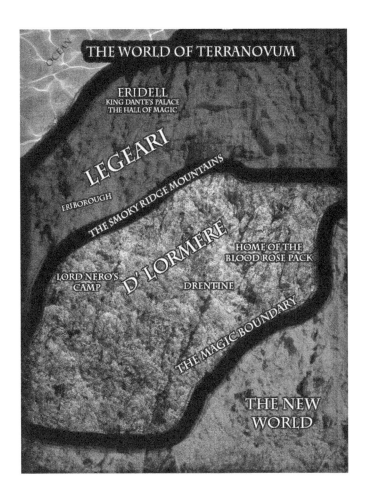

Made in the USA
Middletown, DE
23 August 2020